"Why did you lead me on, Candy?" Nick demanded, his onyx eyes burning into hers.

"Not for revenge," she whispered.

"Then why, Candy?"

Her heart seemed to stop beating. He was so close to her, close enough for her to feel the heat emanating from his hard, masculine frame.

"Nick." His name escaped from her throat in a husky whisper and she tried to move closer. Desire, sharp as a stiletto, sliced through her. She wanted to lose herself in his arms, to feel his hot, hard mouth take hers. She gazed at him with undisguised yearning.

But Nick wouldn't let her close the gap between them. He held her wrists, controlling her movements and keeping her anchored in place. "Tell me, Candy." His voice was deep and low.

Hunger and need rippled through her, intensified by the frustration he was inducing by holding her away from him. A hot spear of sexual excitement rendered her breathless, and she began to tremble. Her body was conditioned to the pleasure and fulfillment she'd known with Nick. It was always like this with him, she thought. Only with him. . . .

WHAT ARE *LOVESWEPT* ROMANCES?

They are stories of true romance and touching emotion. We believe those two very important ingredients are constants in our highly sensual and very believable stories in the *LOVESWEPT* line. Our goal is to give you, the reader, stories of consistently high quality that may sometimes make you laugh, sometimes make you cry, but are always fresh and creative and contain many delightful surprises within their pages.

Most romance fans read an enormous number of books. Those they truly love, they keep. Others may be traded with friends and soon forgotten. We hope that each *LOVESWEPT* romance will be a treasure—a "keeper." We will always try to publish

LOVE STORIES YOU'LL NEVER FORGET
BY AUTHORS YOU'LL ALWAYS REMEMBER

The Editors

LOVESWEPT® • 261

Barbara Boswell
Baby, Baby

BANTAM BOOKS
TORONTO • NEW YORK • LONDON • SYDNEY • AUCKLAND

BABY, BABY

A Bantam Book / June 1988

*If you would be interested in receiving protective vinyl
covers for your Loveswept books, please write to this address
for information:*

Loveswept
Bantam Books
P.O. Box 985
Hicksville, NY 11802

ISBN 0-553-21904-9

Published simultaneously in the United States and Canada

*Bantam Books are published by Bantam Books, a division
of Bantam Doubleday Dell Publishing Group, Inc. Its trademark, consisting of the words "Bantam Books" and the
portrayal of a rooster, is Registered in U.S. Patent and
Trademark Office and in other countries. Marca Registrada.
Bantam Books, 666 Fifth Avenue, New York, New York 10103.*

PRINTED IN THE UNITED STATES OF AMERICA

O   11 10 9 8 7 6 5 4 3 2

One

Babyland, which billed itself as "the only department store dedicated exclusively to serving baby's needs," was a success from the day it opened its doors in Rockville, Maryland. Almost everyone who had a baby or was expecting one seemed to end up there eventually, at least to look if not to buy.

The store had become a topic of conversation in the Washington, D.C. area. There was an entire floor for furniture, ranging from old-fashioned brass cribs to new-age lucite-and-chrome "sleep centers." The clothing floor held just as broad a range in baby and toddler fashions, from practical cotton layette items to tiny rhinestone-studded blue jeans. There was a photography studio, and the Infant Gourmet Boutique on the third floor, where baby could be photographed and/or treated to a wide assortment of palate-pleasing delights— all natural and totally nutritious, of course. And the fourth floor held an incredible selection of toys that promised to educate, stimulate, and entertain Babyland's young patrons, from newborn to preschooler.

Watching her two young nephews, four-year-old Scotty Wickwire and his two-year-old brother Brandon, exuberantly try out the drum sets and bang on the miniature baby grand piano in the Music Land section of

Toyland, Candy Flynn decided that perhaps certain toys were *too* stimulating and entertaining.

"Maybe I'm stifling two potential musical geniuses, but my eardrums have had it," she said aloud to the infant she was holding in her arms. The baby was wearing a pink dress, pink tights, and pink cloth shoes. A pink sweater was draped across Candy's arm. There could be no mistaking this baby for a boy.

"Shall we rout your cousins into Teddy Bear Land?" Candy asked. "It's much quieter there. I hope," she added, and the baby gave her a wide, toothless grin, as if she understood and was amused by it all.

Candy felt the warmth of maternal pride fill every fiber of her being. "Such a beautiful smile. Such a precious girl," she said softly to the baby as she beamed down at her. The baby made a happy, chirping sound and waved her tiny arms, responding fully to the attention.

It was a private moment between mother and child, but everyone who observed the exchange smiled . . . everyone except the dark-haired man standing a few feet away. He shifted the blond baby girl he held from one arm to the other, his onyx eyes fastened on Candy.

The intensity of his stare seemed to have a magnetic effect. Candy turned her head, and her dark green eyes collided with his. Her heart lurched crazily. For one timeless moment, the smiling salesclerks and customers in Babyland seemed to fade into a background haze—even the din her nephews were creating with the toy instruments was muted—as Candy stood trapped in that dark, dark gaze she knew so well.

Nick Torchia. A sweeping tide of hot memories ripped through her. It was suddenly difficult to breathe.

The two baby girls simultaneously broke the spell. The infant in her arms sneezed. The toddler in Nick's arms pointed to a big red balloon tied to a cash register and made a lurch for it.

Candy's attention instantly focused on her child.

"Bless you," she said, and the baby beamed up at her, responding to the familiar sound of her voice.

"Whose baby is she?"

The deep, masculine tones sounded in Candy's ears. She turned slowly to the man who now stood at her side. "Mine," she said, and heard the challenge in her voice. She strove to suppress it. It was important that she respond simply, casually. She instantly mocked herself for the thought. When had her responses to Nick ever been simple or casual? "She's five months old today," she added with a brilliant, false smile.

Out of the corner of her eye she saw Nick tighten his jaw. The little blonde in his arms, dressed in lavender from head to toe, turned her attention from the balloon to Candy and grinned at her, showing off four small, pearly-white teeth.

Candy smiled back at her, and this time her smile was genuine. Who could resist that winsome baby grin and those bright blue eyes, that mop of golden curls? "What an adorable little girl," she said, meaning it. "How old is she?"

"This is my daughter Nichole," Nick said tersely. "I spell her name with an *h* because she's named for me, and Nicholas has an *h* in it. Her nickname is Nicki, and she's fourteen months old."

Nick's child. That gave her pause. A surfeit of emotion threatened to overwhelm her. But because she'd had a lifetime of concealing and denying her feelings, because she was adept at mimicking what she knew to be the correct and socially polite thing to do or say while masking her own raging emotions, Candy successfully composed her features into a polite, social smile. "She's a beautiful child," she said, making the requisite response.

She took a deep breath and proceeded to answer him in kind. "My baby's name is Victoria, after—uh—the grand old queen. Her nickname is Tori."

"And she's five months old?" Nick stared down at the baby snuggled in Candy's arms. Little Tori gazed up at him with round blue eyes. The wisps of hair on her small head were very fair.

His glance swept over Candy's smooth, shoulder-length, sable-brown hair, her deep green eyes. His gaze lowered to encompass the alluring shapeliness of her figure, displayed to perfection by her slim off-white skirt, rose silk blouse, and rose leather high-heeled shoes. Her sense of style was superb; she'd always known how to dress, even back in the days when expensive clothes like these were far beyond her reach. He wondered if what she was wearing under her clothes was as feminine and elegantly sexy as her outer garments.

His body began to tighten involuntarily, and he took a quick gulp of air. "The baby is so fair. Not at all like you," he said bluntly.

Candy treated him to the same type of frank inspection, gazing pointedly at his thick, dark hair and the glittering black irises of his eyes, at his straight Roman nose which she knew had been broken at least once. He was wearing a dark green polo shirt and well-fitting khaki slacks, the type of casual clothing that emphasized the hard, muscular strength of his frame.

She determinedly tore her eyes away from him to stare at the dainty, blond, blue-eyed child he held in his arms. Her tiny nose was cute and upturned, and hopefully would never be altered in a street fight.

"Nichole doesn't look anything like you," Candy retorted, her green eyes suddenly blazing. "She looks like your wife."

"I'm not married, Candace."

She heard the challenge in his voice and forced herself to meet his dark, unwavering gaze. "Neither am I," she replied coolly.

Scotty and Brandon chose that moment to join them, bringing with them a pair of cymbals. The resounding crash caused Tori to start visibly, and Nicki to squeal with delight.

"Will you buy these for us, Aunt Candy?" cried Scotty. "Please!"

"Pease!" echoed Brandon urgently.

"Do you guys remember the whistles I bought you a couple months ago?" Candy asked dryly. "The ones your mom and dad threw out the next day? Well, they probably would like these cymbals just about as much as they liked the whistles. Which is to say, not at all," she added.

"Not at all," echoed Scotty, getting her point.

"Put the cymbals back and we'll go look at the toy trains in Train Land," Candy suggested, and Scotty rushed off to do her bidding, his little brother trailing faithfully at his heels.

"*Aunt* Candy?" Nick repeated, staring from Candy to the two little boys, who already had dumped the cymbals and taken up with a xylophone. "Are you really their aunt?"

Candy nodded. "They're Shay's children. She's expecting another baby in a few weeks. She and her husband are downstairs looking at nursery furniture. The kids got bored, so I brought them up here."

"Shay's kids?" Nick smiled for the first time. "Little Shay is married and a mother?" He shook his head, his smile deepening. "It doesn't seem possible. Whenever I think of your sister Shay, I still picture a cute little kid with great big blue eyes hitting me up for candy and motorcycle rides."

Candy smiled warmly. The memories he evoked were fond ones for her. She'd always adored her younger sister. "Well, Shay still has the great big blue eyes and the sweet tooth, but she's definitely given up motorcycle rides."

"Especially in her current condition, I bet." Nick felt the inevitable, irresistible attraction Candy held for him rise to explosive awareness within him. It always happened when she smiled at him in that particular way, he recalled grimly, from the very first moment they'd met as sophomores in Detroit's Hoover High School all those years ago.

An alarm sounded silently in his head. After all these years, after all they'd been through—after all she'd put him through time after time, he amended resolutely. To look at her now and know that she could still knock him sideways with just a smile.

It was a devastating revelation. His arms tightened reflexively around little Nichole. Oh, no, he told himself, not him. Not anymore. He'd gone too many rounds with Candace Flynn in the past, and he'd lost every one. He was a father now, and she was a mother.

His eyes were drawn compulsively to the infant she held in her arms. Candy's child. Not his baby but another man's. He was unprepared for the intensity of the pain that shot through him, but not surprised by it. He'd been enthralled by her for far too long to expect to be unaffected by the sight of her child. Her child by another man . . .

A stab of sheer, primitive jealousy slashed through him.

Candy felt his eyes upon her, saw him study Tori, and instinctively knew he was in pain. His face betrayed no emotion whatsoever, his usually expressive dark eyes were shuttered, but she still knew what he was feeling, because she had some sort of sixth sense where Nick Torchia was concerned. It gave her a power over him which she knew he resented; what he probably didn't realize was that he was the one person in the world who held a similar power over her.

He was the one man she'd never been able to banish from her thoughts, the only man she had ever cried over. She'd cared for him so intensely that the strength and depth of her feelings had terrified her, and her fear had always compelled her to drive him away. He came too close; he touched her too deeply, he reached her on a level that no one else ever had. She always felt too threatened by the intimacy and inevitably, invariably, pulled away from him.

She knew she'd hurt him in the past. Most of the time it hadn't been intentional, but she'd hurt him badly just the same. He had loved her, and she had been raised to view herself as inherently unlovable. They'd never been able to overcome that basic, deeply divisive conflict and all the problems that had sprung from it.

Tori made a gurgling sound, and Candy's gaze shifted instantly to the infant. Having captured her attention, the baby smiled up at her, her big blue eyes filled with love and trust. The demands, responsibilities, and joys of caring for a child had been a revelation for Candy. She loved every minute of it and knew she was a good mother. Slowly, finally, she was coming to believe that perhaps she wasn't so inherently unlovable, after all.

Candy lifted her eyes to Nick's. He was staring at her. How many times over the years had she seen him look at her with that same watchful stare, which was half admiration and half frustration? She drove him crazy, he'd said so many times. And no wonder, she thought. Poor Nick, he'd definitely had the worst of her, yet for some inexplicable reason he always had come back to her, always had given her another chance. Why did he love her? she'd pondered time and again. How *could* he love her?

She never had been able to fathom it, just as she never had been able to resist taking up with him again and again. Her pulses jumped. She'd last seen him at their high-school reunion, nearly three years ago, when he'd introduced her to the woman he said he intended to marry, the woman who had become Nichole's mother, the woman to whom he was no longer married—

A sudden, incredible thought struck her. Since that time she'd managed to exorcise so many demons that had tormented her in the past. She was a very different woman today, she knew it. How would Nick respond to her now, as a woman who was finally learning how to accept love?

Nick abruptly dragged his eyes away from her. As

ever, he was attuned to her every nuance. And the way she was staring at him—

"No way." He spoke his thoughts aloud. "Forget it, Candy."

"What do you mean?" she asked, startled by the fierceness in his tone.

"I've seen that particular gleam in your eye before, and it invariably means disaster for me. But not this time, baby. I am out of your life, and I intend to stay out. Permanently."

Candy frowned. "I don't recall inviting you into it. In fact, I haven't said a word for the past few minutes."

"You forget how well I know you, Candace. I can practically hear you thinking. And your thoughts go something like this: 'Hey, it's good old Nick. Good old *available* Nick. Haven't seen him in a while. I think I'll jerk him around again.' "

"I wasn't thinking any such thing," Candy said, her temper flaring.

He gave a short laugh. "No? And the fact that Sherrie and I are no longer married hasn't crossed your judicious little mind even once?"

"Sherrie? Oh, yes, your wife," Candy recalled with a disdainful sniff. "The blond bimbo. I warned you it would never last. I mean, she was pretty and sexy, of course, but undeniably vapid. You—"

"Sherrie's dead," Nick interrupted flatly. "She was killed in a car accident a year ago."

Candy gasped. "Dead?" she echoed, truly shocked by the news. *Dead?* "But—but that's terrible! She—she was so young, so beautiful."

"So vapid," Nick reminded her, and Candy flushed scarlet. Her eyes flicked to pretty little blond Nichole in Nick's arms. "I didn't know. Oh, God, Nick, for your baby to have lost her mother so young . . . it's tragic. It must have been awful for you. I'm so sorry."

He gazed at her squarely. "Spare me your urgent avowals of sympathy, Candy. The truth is that neither Nichole nor I miss her at all."

"That's a terrible thing to say!" exclaimed Candy. "Nick, the girl is dead, for heaven's sake!"

His lips twisted into a wry smile. "What a hypocrite you are, Candace. You couldn't stand Sherrie when she was alive. You disliked her on sight and didn't change your mind about her until this moment, when you learned that she happened to be dead."

Candy wasn't sure how to reply to that. She mulled over his cavalier attitude toward the dead woman who had been his wife. She knew Nick well enough to understand how deeply his emotions ran, how very much he cared for those he loved. Obviously he did not love the late, unlamented Sherrie. Candy reprimanded herself sternly for the unmistakable relief that flowed through her. And fixed Nick with her most forbidding courtroom stare. "You certainly don't sound like a grieving husband. The poor girl was the mother of your only child, after all."

"I'll always be grateful to Sherrie for giving birth to Nichole," Nick conceded, "although her role as a mother was brief and could best be described as strictly biological. But I'm not a grieving husband, and I see no reason to pretend that I am. Our marriage was over the moment Sherrie found out she was pregnant and insisted on an abortion. She didn't like the idea of losing her figure, she said. She just knew that being pregnant wasn't going to be any fun."

"And having fun was very important to Sherrie," Candy guessed.

"Having fun was paramount to Sherrie," he confirmed in a dry, clipped tone. "Forget love and responsibility and any other virtue of maturity. Sherrie opted for fun every time. Fun and money."

"Oh, Nick," Candy said softly, lowering her eyes. "How did you talk her into going through with the pregnancy and having the baby?"

"I paid her. She demanded cold, hard cash, and I gave it to her. And then she flew to Mexico for a quickie divorce a month after the baby was born," he added with a shrug.

"Good Lord, Nick, in all the divorce cases I handled in my practice before I was appointed to family court, I never had anyone who had to *pay* a spouse to bear a child. And to file for divorce just a month after giving birth—"

"Sherrie wanted to file two weeks earlier," Nick interrupted dryly. "I convinced her to wait out the month for propriety's sake."

"What about custody of the baby? How was that decided?"

"The question of custody was never an issue." Nick gave his head a wry shake. "Sherrie would've been aghast if I'd suggested that she take Nichole even for an occasional weekend. A child would have severely cramped her style." He grimaced. "She was celebrating her freedom six weeks after the divorce with a high roller in Vegas. The blood-alcohol levels for her and her friend far exceeded the legal driving limits. There were traces of cocaine found as well."

"Dammit, Nick, I told you she was all wrong for you," Candy said indignantly. She was outraged on his behalf. "I knew from the moment I met her that she was a trampy little airhead on the make, that she wasn't good enough for you and never would be. I tried to talk some sense into you, but you were so damn stubborn. I—I'm sorry you were hurt."

"Sherrie didn't hurt me. She couldn't," Nick said coolly. "You have to love someone to be hurt by them, and I didn't love Sherrie."

"Then why in the hell did you marry her?" Candy demanded.

"I tried to explain it to you the night of the reunion, Candace, although I was aware that you weren't really listening at the time."

No, she hadn't been listening, Candy agreed silently. She'd been reeling with shock at his bald pronouncement. Nick, thinking of marrying? She knew she would never forget the stunning pain she'd felt upon hearing that news. No, her heart had screamed, it was unthinkable, unbearable. She'd spent the rest of the night in a heartbroken daze and had cried herself to sleep for weeks afterward. Nick, married! She was unable to suppress the small shiver that coursed through her at the memory of that awful time. Not that she'd revealed anything of what she'd felt to anyone. Candace Flynn was not one to wear her heart on her sleeve. She'd borne her pain alone, hiding behind her facade of indomitable strength.

She faced him now, her green gaze cool and unwavering. She wasn't about to reveal how she'd felt about his marriage now, either. "Suppose you refresh my memory, Nick. Exactly what were your reasons for marrying?"

Nick heaved a sigh. "I'd decided that it was finally time for me to marry, and Sherrie seemed a suitable enough choice. I thought we would deal well together. She was young and lovely, quite amiable and compliant. She had no temper to speak of; nothing ever seemed to phase her."

Candy gave him an arch look. "I believe the word you're looking for is *shallow*. I've seen the type. Whatever happens, however tragic or moving or joyful, their reaction is always a bland, 'Oh, wow.' "

"Did I mention that Sherrie held no strong opinions?" Nick asked silkily. "That she wasn't stubborn or impatient or rigid or argumentative, and that she didn't have a compulsion to be in constant control?"

"And you were bored silly with her, weren't you?" Candy shot back. "You admit that you didn't love her. You only married her because you were in the throes of what the popular press calls a mid-life crisis."

Nick shrugged. "Trite as it sounds, I suppose it's true. I'd reached a level of success in my business that exceeded my wildest dreams, but I decided that I needed more than work in my life. I wanted a home, a family, a child to nurture and love. I believe the current term for the feeling is a need for generativity. You must have experienced something similar when you decided to have a baby, Candy."

She wasn't about to go into that. Not with Nick, who would never leave the topic alone if he sensed that she was hiding something. And she was. Oh, dear heaven, she certainly was!

So she did what came naturally, based on years of skillfully won courtroom battles—she seized the offensive. "We're not talking about me, we're talking about you," she said in an aggressively prosecutorial style, "and why you married a blond idiot that you met on an airplane. On an airplane, for God's sake!" she added crossly. "Did you check your brains before boarding?"

"You were just as incensed the night of the reunion, when I introduced you to Sherrie and told you I was thinking about marrying her," Nick recalled with a slight smile. "And I remember telling you that if you wanted to save me from what you termed a 'marital catastrophe with a vacuous nitwit who was totally unsuitable for me,' then you could marry me yourself."

Candy averted her eyes. "Don't, Nick," she said softly, her voice quavering with uncharacteristic nervousness.

Except that it wasn't uncharacteristic for her to be nervous around Nick. He was the one person in the entire universe who could induce jitters in the normally unflappable Candace Flynn. He was always so blunt, so open and frank. And he knew her far too well. She was painfully aware of hot color suffusing her cheeks. Nick Torchia was also the only person, living or dead, who'd ever made cool, cool Candy blush.

She took a deep, steadying breath, determined to regain her lost composure. "You manage to make the most outrageous remarks!" She tried for a commanding scorn, but her voice was weak, not at all what she'd intended.

"I speak my mind, which is tough for someone with your penchant for secrecy, subterfuge, and self-deception to handle," Nick returned smoothly. "You're blushing,

Candace. Why, I wonder? We're both fully aware that my proposal to you that night was merely one of the many that I had made to you over the years. However, that one happens to be especially memorable to me because it was the final one."

She knew she shouldn't respond to such a remark. He was deliberately trying to bait her, to rattle her. And he'd succeeded, thoroughly. As usual. "I'm sure I don't know what you're talking about," she heard herself say shakily.

"I mean that I've made my last proposal of marriage, to you or to anyone else. I've had it with marriage, it obviously isn't for me. I have my work and my child, and that's enough. It would be greedy to ask for anything more."

"That mistake with Sherrie can hardly be defined as a marriage," Candy felt compelled to point out.

"I thought it fit your definition of marriage perfectly, Candace. I thought you considered every marriage a major mistake."

"Not anymore. Nick, I've changed," she blurted out urgently, impulsively. Another radical departure in behavior for her. Judge Flynn was *not* given to urgent, impulsive statements. But she couldn't seem to stop herself. "My views have changed in so many ways, Nick. I've watched my sister's marriage grow stronger over the years. And after my brother married and I saw how good it is between him and his wife, I began to believe that maybe, just maybe, certain marriages *can* work."

She paused, suddenly breathless. "And now, loving Tori the way I do, I think I've finally learned that it's possible for people to change and be changed by loving and to—"

"I'm glad your sister and brother are happily married, and I'm glad you have a child that you love," Nick interrupted swiftly. "But I'm not going to get involved with you again, Candy. And I'm sure as hell not going to ask you to marry me again."

"I wasn't asking you to!" Candy bristled. Her face felt hot; her whole body was one heated blush.

Nick gave a sardonic laugh. "Weren't you, Candace?" he said softly, tauntingly.

Was she? Candy's heart turned over in her chest. "No," she insisted, even as a jolt of electricity flashed through her. She couldn't take her eyes away from him, and her gaze swept over his hard, muscular, six-foot frame, his broad shoulders and strong arms, his narrow hips and long, trim legs. Her mouth felt dry. He had been her first lover. The first and only man she'd ever loved.

In that moment it all swept over her again, the hot confusion and the restless passion she knew only with Nick. The burning intensity that made her grow weak and start to tremble whenever he took her in his arms. A potent combination of fear and excitement spun through her. No other man could arouse the swift, wild needs in her that Nick did. Only Nick could make her lose her rigid, repressive self-control. She'd been able to dominate every other man she'd ever met, but she'd never been able to dominate Nick. She remembered how it was between them, how it had always been, how he would draw her out of herself and make her let go. . . .

Nick saw the look in her eyes and read it for what it was. Her lips parted softly, reflexively, and he felt the physical effects of that small gesture deep within him. He groaned inwardly. This was madness, a sweet, wild madness that he knew far too well. He steeled himself against it, against her.

"No," he said firmly, turning away from her. "It's all over between us, Candy. We're two mature adults, we each have a child, and I'm finished with your push-pull, avoidance-approach, I-want-you-go-away style."

"You're right, Nick." She stared at him. "That's exactly what I do. Not consciously, but—"

"I know, I know. I could write a book on you and the colossal terror and allure getting close holds for you.

You've been at war with yourself for as long as I can remember, and I've jumped into the battle too many times." He smiled almost gently. "You're a very complex lady, Candace Flynn. The most fascinating and the most difficult woman I've ever known, but I've reached the stage in my life where I want things simple and easy. I'm opting out this time around, honey."

Candy was shaken by the finality in Nick's tone. He didn't want her anymore, she thought numbly. It had taken her years to do it, but she'd finally killed every vestige of his feelings for her.

Little Nichole chose that moment to squirm restlessly in her father's arms. "She wants down," guessed Nick.

"Does she walk yet?" Candy asked, blindly turning her attention to Nichole.

"She learned to walk last month, and it's still a thrill to her," Nick said, smiling indulgently at his daughter. "It's all she wants to do."

He set Nichole on her feet, and the little girl started off cautiously, walking with a wide gait toward the noise of Music Land. "Nicki," Nick called, hovering over her. "Be careful, sweetheart. Don't fall."

He was definitely a protective father, Candy thought, smiling through the tears that welled up unexpectedly in her eyes. She determinedly blinked them away.

She remembered how kind and patient Nick had been with her little sister Shay all those years ago, when Nick Torchia and Candy Flynn were Hoover High's hottest, most tempestuous couple. He'd never complained when Candy insisted on dragging Shay along on some of their dates because she didn't want to leave the little girl behind with their unpredictable, often drunk, and forever battling parents.

With a tightness in her throat she remembered how much she genuinely liked Nick. When she wasn't hungering for him as a lover or pushing him away as an intimate threat, she'd always liked and enjoyed him as a close, dear friend.

Firmly suppressing her emotions, she called to her nephews and suggested that they take Nichole to Teddy Bear Land to see the enormous collection of teddy bears on sale there. Scotty and Brandon each took one of Nichole's hands, and the little girl laughed up at them, pleased to be with other children.

"Nichole is very friendly," Candy murmured as she and Nick followed the trio. Though the child was a stranger to her, she felt oddly connected to her. "She's not at all shy."

Nick nodded, his eyes on his small daughter. And then his gaze swung back to Candy and her child. "Are you going to let me hold her?" he asked softly, touching his long finger to Tori's hand. Her tiny fingers closed around it. Nick and Candy stared into each other's eyes for a long, silent moment.

Carefully Candy handed the baby to him. She watched him enfold the small body in his hands, watched him smile as he held the baby upright against his chest. Tori's little fists grasped the dark cotton of his shirt. Nick spoke softly to her, and she cooed with pleasure.

"She—she's not used to men," Candy offered hesitantly. She made a mental note to get her brother, Case, and brother-in-law, Adam, Tori's two uncles, more involved as the child grew older.

"What about her father?" Nick's voice held an edge of sharpness. "Isn't he in the picture at all?"

Candy shook her head.

"Who is he, Candace?"

"Nick, please, I'd rather not discuss it."

Nick shifted the baby so her little head bobbed over his shoulder. She looked around, wide-eyed, clearly pleased with the new perspective this position offered. And with the unfamiliar masculine strength as well? Candy stared at the sight of Nick's big hands holding the baby so competently, so firmly, yet so tenderly. Her heart seemed to jump into her throat.

"Who is your baby's father, Candy?" Nick persisted,

undaunted by her refusal to answer. "And why are you raising this child alone?"

Candy didn't look at him. "Suppose I told you that he was a big, blond surfer? The male equivalent of Sherrie. Would you call off the interrogation?"

"No, because I wouldn't believe you."

"Why not? You had a child by a blond bimbo. Why shouldn't I have one by a blond bozo?"

"Dammit, Candace, if you wanted a child, why"—he paused and inhaled deeply—"why didn't you come to me?"

Two

Candy didn't remember taking the few steps that brought her so close to him, but she must have, for suddenly she was standing next to him, her body nearly touching his. Vibrations, tangibly intense, hummed between them. Her hand slipped hesitantly into the crook of his arm, and she gazed up at him. The blood was thundering in her ears. "Nick, I—"

"Aunt Candy, Mommy and Daddy are coming up those magic stairs!" Scotty raced up to them, announcing the arrival of his parents at the top of his lungs. Then he whirled around and ran toward the escalator to greet them.

Candy nearly snatched Tori from Nick's arms as she swiftly moved away from him. She watched Brandon and Nichole toddle over to him, still holding hands. When Nick bent to pick up his daughter, the little boy held up his arms. "Up too," he demanded. With a shrug and a smile Nick scooped up Brandon in his other arm.

Candy turned away. The sight of Nick holding the two children was an especially evocative one for her. Shay and her husband, Adam Wickwire, were stepping off the escalator. Keeping a firm arm around Shay, Adam took Scotty's hand.

As the trio walked toward them, Candy noticed that Adam's expression was oddly grim. Scotty was chattering on, but neither of his parents appeared to be listening to him. And Shay . . . Candy felt her heart plunge to the pit of her stomach. One look at her younger sister's face confirmed that something was very wrong.

She hurried toward them. "Shay, what is it?" she demanded tensely, her green eyes meeting her sister's deep blue ones. "What's wrong?"

"I'm in labor," Shay murmured.

"What?" Candy gasped. "But you can't be! It's too early. The baby isn't due for another two or three weeks."

"The baby has other ideas," Adam said calmly. "Fortunately we're not far from the hospital. I'm going to take Shay there now." Shay grimaced and bit her lower lip, and his arm tightened around her. "Candy, will you take Scotty and Brandon home and stay with them?" he asked.

"Of course," Candy said automatically. But she couldn't tear her gaze away from Shay's face. Her little sister was in pain! And trying bravely not to show it. Anxiety and concern made Candy's insides churn.

She tried to swallow, but her throat was too dry. "Shay, don't worry. Everything is going to be all right," she said, assuming her role as omnipotent older sister. But her voice was a choked, tense whisper.

Shay nodded and managed a smile. "I know, Candy. Don't *you* worry."

Candy fought the urge to weep. "I'll take the boys," she began, then turned and bumped into Nick, who must have joined them at some point, although she wasn't aware of when. He still held Brandon and Nichole in his arms. "I'm taking the boys home," she said in a high, strained voice that she hardly recognized as her own. "Adam is taking Shay to the hospital."

"Nick Torchia?" Shay spotted Nick, and a sudden, bright smile lit her face. "Oh, Nick, I can't believe it's you! It's been years!" She stepped forward to give him a quick hug at the same moment that another contraction took her breath away. She leaned heavily into Adam. "I guess it's kind of an inopportune time for a reunion," she said wryly.

"I guess it is, little Shay-bird," Nick said fondly, using the old nickname he'd bestowed upon her so many years ago. "I already met your boys. This must be your husband."

"Yes," Shay said, blinking back emotional tears. She introduced him to Adam. "Nick was my hero when I was little," she explained, her dark blue eyes shining with nostalgic pleasure. "He used to take me on motorcycle rides and give me candy from his family's store. I had pizza for the first time at Nick's house when I was six years old." She smiled first at Adam, then Nick. "I've yet to taste any pizza as good as your mother's, Nick."

"I'll be sure to tell her that," Nick said. "She'll be delighted to hear it."

"What brings you to the D.C. area, Nick?" Shay asked. She cast a quick, speculative glance at Candy. "Are you living here now?"

"Temporarily," he replied. "I'm opening a branch office of my security consulting firm here. Our headquarters is in Los Angeles."

"Torch Security Incorporated," Candy inserted with a note of pride. "TSI. Nick founded it and has been very successful."

Shay looked as if she would have liked to ask more, but Adam spoke up. "Darling, we'd better leave now." She drew a sudden, sharp breath and clutched his arm, nodding weakly.

Scotty accepted his parents' departure with a solemn nod, but Brandon burst into tears the moment his mother kissed him good-bye. As Adam and Shay stepped onto the escalator, Tori, perhaps responding to Candy's own tension, started to howl. Nichole stared at Brandon, then at Tori, and began to wail too.

Scotty covered his ears with his hands. "Too noisy," he said with a scowl. But his lower lip quivered.

Candy felt on the verge of panic. If Scotty cried, she was sunk. He was old enough to know that something was wrong, and she had no idea what to say to him. Tori was bellowing, her small body stiff with rage. Brandon's cries were piercing, but thankfully Nick was holding him. Nick . . . Her eyes met his.

"Help," she said softly in a shaky attempt at humor. "I think I'm in over my head."

Nick stared down at her. His earlier vow to stay away from her, to keep firmly and irrevocably out of her life, flashed briefly to mind. And was instantly dismissed as all his protective instincts emerged in full force. He couldn't leave her alone with three unhappy small children, especially not when he knew how worried she was about Shay. He could guess how the sight of Shay in pain must have affected her. Candy had never been able to bear to see her little sister distressed, he remembered, thinking back to those long-ago days in Detroit. Even as a teenager he'd found her selfless devotion to her younger sister one of her most admirable and endearing qualities.

"I'll help you with the kids," he said, and told himself that he wasn't bowing to the inevitable, he was merely doing a good turn for an old friend.

The Wickwires lived in the exclusive Maryland suburb of Potomac in a spacious and elegant Tudor-style house to which a substantial addition recently had been built to accommodate the growing family.

"It seems so odd being here without Shay and Adam." Candy spoke her thoughts aloud as she gave Tori a bottle of warm formula. Nichole sat beside her on the cushioned glider on the screened patio, holding a baby bottle to the lips of the large-size doll she held in her lap. She babbled a string of syllables.

Candy couldn't help but grin at the child. "I think we

need an interpreter here, Nicki. I don't speak your language, and you don't speak English."

Despite her anxiety over Shay, she found Nick's small blond daughter an amusing diversion. For her own one-year-old reasons, Nichole had taken a liking to Candy. While Candy changed Tori's diapers, Nichole had attempted a similar action on the big baby doll Nick had bought her at Babyland that afternoon. He'd bought one for Tori, too, although the doll was the size of the baby herself, and it would be months before she could play with it.

Candy's eyes drifted to the two pairs of cymbals that lay on the ground. Scotty and Brandon had cheered up the moment Nick announced that he wanted to buy each of them a present. Her gaze continued beyond the patio, to the large, lush green lawn where Nick was watching Scotty and assisting Brandon on the wooden jungle gym and swing set.

"Oh, Nichole, I don't know what I would have done without your daddy today," Candy said, and sighed.

"Da!" Nichole exclaimed eagerly.

"We're definitely communicating now, aren't we, Nicki? We both know who we're talking about." Candy smiled at Nichole, then stared down at Tori, whose large, dark blue eyes watched her intently.

Shay had those same beautiful deep blue eyes, fringed by long; dark lashes, Candy thought, and she was struck by an intense feeling of déjà vu. She vividly remembered being ten years old and sitting on the shabby sofa in the Flynn family's cramped Detroit apartment, feeding a bottle to the infant Shay, who had watched her as closely as baby Tori was watching her now.

She remembered making a silent promise to love and protect her baby sister, and she'd always tried to keep it. She'd made the same vow the night she'd taken the howling little newborn Tori in her arms, and the infant had stopped crying and stared at her, as if sensing that she was safe at last.

Tori finished her bottle, and Candy placed her in the beribboned bassinet that had been used by Scotty and Brandon and was awaiting the third Wickwire child. Candy felt a sudden rush of emotion as she thought of her sister. Oh, Shay, please be all right, she implored silently. And then Nichole, who had followed her inside, planted a tender kiss on her doll's cheek before unceremoniously dropping it on its head. Candy couldn't help but laugh at the one-year-old's style of mothering.

"What's so funny?" Nick stood in the doorway, staring at her.

"Your daughter," Candy said, and picked up the little girl. "I'm glad she's here, she makes me laugh."

Nick didn't tell her how good it made him feel to hear her laugh. He didn't mention how the sight of his child in her arms moved him. He didn't dare. He wasn't about to start something when he already knew how it would end. With both of them angry and hurt. That's how it always ended between them.

He cleared his throat. "I thought I'd make the kids some hot dogs for dinner and then give them a bath and put them to bed. Any house with kids over a year old in it has hot dogs in the refrigerator," he added knowingly.

He was right, and confidently proceeded to microwave hot dogs for Scotty, Brandon, and Nichole. Candy opened a jar of applesauce and spooned some onto each plate. The children had a good time at dinner. The two younger ones imitated Scotty's every action, then all three roared with laughter. Nick and Candy sat at the table with them, slightly bewildered by all the noisy hilarity.

"Three sure seems like a lot of kids, doesn't it?" Nick remarked as he scooped vanilla ice cream into three plastic dishes. "Shay is really going to have her hands full."

"She'll manage. Shay is great with kids. She never loses her cool," said Candy with a smile. "And Adam is a marvelous father. Like you," she added impulsively.

Nick methodically placed a dish of ice cream and a

spoon before each child. And then he turned slowly to Candy. "I'm not sure how to respond, Candace. Compliments from you are so rare. This may be a first, in fact, and I find myself questioning your motives."

"I don't have any ulterior motive, Nick. I meant what I said. You love Nichole and it shows. I—" She dropped her gaze and stared at the tiles on the floor. "I'm trying to become more open, to tell others the good things I like about them. It's been difficult for me to do that in the past, but I'm trying to change."

Was she? Nick wondered as he sank down onto a chair at the table. Or was she trying to work her way through the defenses he'd built against her? Oh, she was an expert when it came to gauging his feelings, he thought grimly. She'd always known exactly what to say and do to bring him the most pleasure—and to inflict the most pain.

Candy sat down at the table beside him. They both turned their full attention to the children. Nichole grasped her spoon and inserted it into the dish of ice cream, managing to fill it, although not very well. She then turned the spoon upside down, spilling the contents before it reached her mouth. Candy and Nick both laughed when she resorted to using her fingers instead.

"It's hard to believe that this time next year, Tori will be sitting in a high chair feeding herself," Candy mused.

"It all happens so quickly," said Nick, and sighed wistfully. "It seems like only yesterday that Nichole was Tori's size." He stared silently into space for a long moment. And then asked, "What kind of pregnancy did you have with Tori, Candy? Was it easy or difficult? What kind of labor did you have?"

Candy, who'd picked up Nichole's spoon to help her out, abruptly dropped it. It landed on the table with a clatter. Pleased with the noise, Nichole promptly imitated her actions. Brandon and Scotty followed suit, and there was a gleeful round of giggling. And another round of spoon dropping.

"Monkey see, monkey do," Candy said with a laugh. She was inordinately relieved that the children's antics made sane conversation an impossibility, because Nick's probing questions could easily lead to some dangerous answers. Dangerous for her and for all the Flynns.

There were no more opportunities for him to ask any more of them. The three lively children claimed their complete attention. Nick manfully presided over the long and raucous bathtime. Candy assisted him in tucking the boys into their beds and putting Nichole— wearing a pair of pajamas borrowed from Brandon—in a portable crib in an empty upstairs bedroom.

"Would you like to join me in an adults-only dinner?" Candy asked Nick as they descended the stairs. "I can make us some omelets. All the ingredients are here— tomatoes, green peppers, onions, mushrooms, ham, and cheese. Just the kind you like," she added with a smile.

He knew she was a good cook. She'd prepared many meals for him over the years. "I don't think so," he said, although the promise of the omelet was difficult to resist. "I'll just make myself a peanut butter and jelly sandwich—a house with a kid over a year old in it always has peanut butter and jelly too."

"You don't even like peanut butter and jelly. Why don't you want me to make the omelet, Nick? It's no trouble, honestly."

Nick turned to her with a frown. "Honestly? Okay, let's be honest, Candy. This is getting just a little too close to playing house, and it's making me nervous. We've taken care of the kiddies, and now you're offering to cook for me. An intimate little adult dinner for two. With candlelight, perhaps? And wine? Then what, Candy? Do we turn off the lights, turn on the music, and turn on each other?"

She knew he expected her to jump furiously on the defensive and begin the fight that would end in her throwing him out, if he didn't stomp out first. But she was so tired of that script. They'd overused it so often during the years, it was as if it were set in cement.

They didn't have to play it that way, Candy decided thoughtfully. A different response from her was the first move out of the straitjacket that was their past. "All I suggested was an omelet," she said quietly. Her expression softened. "I don't want to quarrel with you, Nick."

"Why not? Quarreling with me has always been one of your favorite pastimes."

She shook her head. "You've been so kind today. So helpful. But that's nothing new for you, Nick. You've always been kind and helpful to me. I've always known I could depend on you. I've always trusted you." She swallowed and added bravely, "In my own limited way, of course. But that's my problem, not yours."

Nick stared at her, riveted. The Candace Flynn he had known for so long admitted to no weakness or vulnerability. She was defensively aggressive and constantly on guard; dealing with her was something akin to walking through a mine field, anticipating an explosion at any given moment. But this Candy, with her sad green eyes and soft voice, with her attempts at insight and her genuine interest in her daughter and his . . . He gave his head a shake. He had absolutely no idea how to deal with her.

Candy saw the confusion in his troubled black eyes. She didn't blame him for being wary of her. She'd made so many mistakes with him in the past. It was as if she'd been programmed to sabotage any chance she'd ever been given for happiness. Maybe she had been programmed, at that. An unloving mother and a negligent and selfish father had let her know that she hadn't been wanted by either of them long before she reached kindergarten age. And she'd spent the rest of her life trying to prove that no one else could possibly want her, either. Nothing Nick had ever said or done had convinced her otherwise.

She straightened her shoulders and took a deep breath. Nick obviously didn't want her anymore. There was nothing to do but to try to be his friend, although he seemed intent upon rebuffing even the friendship she was attempting to offer.

"I don't have any designs on you, Nick," she said, forcing a nonchalance that she didn't feel. "I'm hungry, and I thought you might be too. If you really want peanut butter, go ahead and have it, but I'm going to make an omelet for myself."

Nick didn't really want peanut butter. The two of them ended up eating their omelets in the oak-paneled family room while watching the news on television. One of the top stories was the upcoming Baby Jay custody trial, which was mentioned on both the local and national broadcasts.

It was a complicated case. Baby Jay, as the child was referred to in court documents, was a six-month-old boy who, since his birth, had lived with the woman who'd contracted with a surrogate to bear him.

Candy, along with most of the nation, was now familiar with the three principals in the case. There was Plaintiff A, the childless widow whose late husband had donated his sperm to conceive Baby Jay. It was she who'd brought the child home from the hospital and taken care of him since then. Plaintiff B was a divorcee who'd donated the egg for the in vitro fertilization. Plaintiff C, a single mother of two, was the surrogate mother of the embryo, which had been implanted in her uterus. Each woman claimed that she had a legal right to the baby, and all wanted the contracts that had been previously drawn up to be set aside.

"I hadn't realized that case was to be decided here in Montgomery County," said Nick, gazing thoughtfully at Candy. "Does that mean that you might be the judge hearing it?"

Candy shrugged noncommittally. "Rumor has it that Roger Wright, our assignments judge in family court, doesn't want to hear the case himself and is leaning toward assigning it to me or Russell Reauveau, a senior judge on the bench. Of course, any one of the family-court judges might be chosen."

"That case is a one-in-a-million career maker for the

judge who presides over it," Nick observed. "It's a natural headline grabber—three different women fighting for custody of a baby, each with a unique claim on the child. The tabloids have already dubbed it the 'Torn Between Three Mothers Case.' "

"I know," said Candy. "It's a test case. High-tech motherhood on trial. And the fact that all three women are single is an additional media hook."

"It'll mean continuing daily press coverage, national recognition, and the chance to be immortalized in textbooks for future generations of law students," Nick said dryly. "Not to mention whatever monetary rewards that can be gleaned later from the lecture circuit, and probable book contracts. I wish you the best of luck in landing the case, Candy."

She frowned, staring pensively into space. She could hardly come right out and say that she didn't want to hear the custody case of the decade. But she didn't, she silently admitted.

Being Candace, she couldn't admit it aloud. Instead, she sent up a cautious trial balloon. "The Baby Jay case is a legal and scientific morass that'll involve an incredible amount of time, both in and out of the courtroom. If I got the case, it would mean I'd have less time with Tori. I have a wonderful baby-sitter who comes to the house while I'm at work, but I want my baby to spend most of her time with me."

"If you're offered the case, you'll take it," Nick predicted with a confidence that set her teeth on edge.

"You think you know me so well." She didn't bother to mask her irritation.

"I do know you, Candace. And that's always bugged you. Scared you too," Nick added pointedly.

"I'm not scared of you," Candy said scoffingly.

"Not physically, no," Nick agreed. "You know I'd never slap you around like your folks did. But you're damn scared of the way I make you feel, and you've spent half your life running away from me because of it."

Candy jumped to her feet, adrenaline rushing through

her veins as she prepared to engage in battle with him. Bringing up her parents was a definite declaration of war. She glanced at him and saw him tense. His expression was somber as he braced himself for her verbal riposte. She always knew exactly what to say to infuriate him the most, and they both were aware of it.

He stood up, and her eyes flicked over him once more. He was standing rigidly erect, his mouth drawn into a taut line. And then she noticed the dark circles under his eyes. He looked so tired, she thought suddenly. Running his security consulting business, overseeing the establishment of the new office, and playing single parent to his baby daughter had to be both demanding and exhausting for him.

Her anger seemed to drain abruptly from her, as if some unseen plug had been pulled. She didn't want to contribute to his tense exhaustion, she realized. She wanted to ease it.

"Nick, I told you that I don't want to fight," she said quietly. "Sit down and finish your coffee."

Nick appeared stunned by her failure to pursue the quarrel. He sat down and hesitantly reached for his coffee cup, his expression showing the incredulity he felt.

"I guess you don't know me as well as you think you do," Candy couldn't resist pointing out.

His brows narrowed and he gazed at her thoughtfully. "Don't I?" He continued to stare at her. "What kind of game are you playing now, Candy?"

"No games." She leaned toward him, her green eyes wide and fixed intently upon him. "Let's simply talk, Nick."

"Small talk, you mean? That's something we've never managed very well with each other, have we? We just plunge straight into intimate and personal issues, like marital status and death and birth . . . which reminds me, you never did answer my questions about—"

"Where are you staying while you're in the area, Nick?" Candy interrupted, taking charge of the conversation.

A typical Candy move. She made it a point to be in charge.

Nick allowed himself to be diverted. "I've rented a house not far from here. Nichole and I will stay until I'm satisfied everything is running smoothly, and then we'll go home to California."

"Tell me about your business," she said, sweetly inviting, and crossing her long, shapely legs as she lounged back against the cushions.

The quietly seductive rustle made by the movement of her thighs, encased in the rose-tinted silk stockings, seemed to echo in his head. He dragged his eyes away from her legs. She had well-shaped calves and slender ankles. In his mind's eye he pictured her smooth, rounded thighs and felt himself grow taut.

"Candy . . ." Nick's voice held a warning note. She knew what she was doing to him, and he knew that she knew. "Stop playing games."

"I told you, I'm not playing games. I want to know all about TSI," she insisted. "Oh, I know that you started your firm in L.A. when you got out of the Marines. I'd just like to know more about what it encompasses. We've never actually talked about it."

"This sounds like one of those get-the-man-to-talk-about-his-work ploys from a how-to-get-a-man book," he said dryly.

"Since you claim to know me so well, you'll have to realize that I would never read one of those books," she retorted. She guessed that his late wife Sherrie had, though. She frowned at the thought of his marriage. "I happen to be genuinely interested in security consulting. Did you make your sources and contacts while you were with naval intelligence in the Marines?"

He nodded. "In the beginning the firm did investigative background checks on candidates for certain government and corporate positions. We still do that sort of thing, but several years ago I branched out into the field of personal security. We run intensive training programs for the chauffeurs and bodyguards of executives and diplomats assigned to foreign countries, and we teach self-defense courses. We also install security systems in buildings and cars. Almost all my employees are former servicemen with experience in intelligence and police work." He smiled slightly. "I've even managed to pick up a college degree along the way. Surprised?"

"Not by your success. I always knew you had what it takes to get ahead. I just wasn't sure how far you wanted to go."

"Maybe you've been the catalyst that's spurred me on," he said lightly. "I've yet to meet anyone as ambitious as you, Candy. From the time we were in high school you were determined to make it. You've certainly succeeded; you must've met every one of your career goals."

"I have, but—" She broke off. Nick was right. She had achieved every goal she'd set for herself—and then some. So how did she explain the unsettling feelings and doubts that churned within her? She'd tried denying them, then ignoring them. Neither tactic had worked. She was both confused and alarmed by this uncharacteristic introspection that had recently begun to plague her.

"But?" prompted Nick.

She knew an overwhelming longing to pour out her heart to him. Nick Torchia was the one person in the world who knew that there was another, different Candy under the arrogant and unshakably cool exterior she presented to the world.

But her guarded reserve went too deep. The walls not only kept others out but also trapped her within. So she shrugged and decided to turn the conversation away from herself. "What made you decide on a college degree, Nick? I remember that it definitely wasn't one of your priorities."

"Back in high school, it wasn't," he agreed. "When you won the scholarship to the University of Michigan and pleaded with me to apply there, too, I was dead set against it. Remember how furious you were with me? You accused me of lacking ambition. You were aghast that I wanted us to get married at eighteen and live in the old neighborhood. That I planned to make a living working in my family's grocery store."

"The thought of spending my whole life in the old neighborhood horrified me," Candy admitted quietly. "I wanted to get as far away from there as I could, and I knew education was the only way out. As much as I"—she lowered her lashes—"as much as I loved you, Nick, it would've been a drastic mistake for us to have married so young." She paused and shuddered. "We probably would've ended up with a marriage like my parents had. Would you have wanted to bring innocent children into a mess like that? What if I'd been the kind of mother my mother was?"

"Your parents were the world's worst," Nick agreed, "but we wouldn't have ended up like them. I saw how loving and protective you were toward your little sister. You'd voluntarily assumed responsibility for Shay long before your mother's death made you her legal guardian. I don't believe for one minute that you'd ever treat a child the way your mother treated you."

"Thanks for the vote of confidence," Candy said softly. "It means a lot. Especially now, since I have Tori. She needs me, and I love taking care of her. I'll never hurt or mistreat her, Nick. I love her."

"I know." His voice was gentle. And then his face hardened, and he drew his mouth into a tight, straight line. "But what about Tori's father? Did he leave you when you learned you were pregnant?" The very idea enraged him. And then another troubling thought struck him. "Or didn't you bother to inform him of his impending fatherhood?"

Candy sighed. "You're not going to let it rest until you get an answer, are you, Nick? You're right, we never do indulge in any polite, social chitchat. We always aim straight for the emotional jugular."

"Answer my questions, Candy."

"I can see why you've been so successful in your line of work. You have a penchant for ferreting out information." She set her coffee aside and faced him. Her heart was pounding, and she drew in a deep, steadying breath.

"Nick, I—I didn't give birth to Victoria. I adopted her five months ago, when she was just four days old."

Three

Nick stared at her, stunned by the information. "You *adopted* her?" he asked, stressing the word. "Why didn't you say so in the first place?"

Candy shrugged. "You didn't ask."

"I didn't ask?" he repeated incredulously. He rose to his feet and glared down at her. "*I didn't ask*?"

"It's true," Candy insisted, using a courtroom tactic that had always served her well in her days as the county's leading divorce lawyer—tossing out a partial, but irrelevant, truth as a diversionary measure. "You never once asked me point-blank if I'd adopted the baby. If you had, I would have said yes."

A streak of fury ricocheted through him. "The reason I never even thought about adoption was because you deliberately fostered the illusion that you'd given birth to her."

Candy swallowed hard. She could deny it, of course. But they would both know she was lying. "I don't expect you to understand," she said, avoiding his accusing black eyes.

"Oh, I understand, Candace. I understand very well. You knew I would find the thought of you bearing another man's child painful, and in your own inimitable way you decided to stick it to me yet again."

"That's not true!" Candy said hotly.

"The hell it isn't! You knew how much I wanted a child with you. It's been a dream of mine for years and years. When we lost our baby—"

"I don't talk about that, Nick. Not with you, not with anyone."

"Oh, I know. You've been adamant about keeping silent on the subject. But I should've made you talk about it. Keeping it locked inside you all these years has been a big mistake."

"It was my choice," Candy said tightly. "And it all happened a long time ago and—and has nothing to do with our lives today."

"Doesn't it, Candace?"

"No, it doesn't!" She glowered at him. "Some people jump to conclusions, but *you* take quantum leaps, Nick Torchia."

"My conclusion is a logical and valid one," Nick said coldly. "Since I'd had a child with another woman, you decided to take revenge by allowing me to believe that you'd had a child by another man." His eyes glittered. "Well, congratulations, honey, you haven't lost your touch. You can still reach me in places that no one else will ever be able to penetrate." He cast a final, dark glare at her and walked away.

She watched him stalk to the door. He was leaving her. Again. The melancholy sadness that washed over her was brutally physical in its impact. She leaned back against the sofa and closed her eyes. She didn't see him stop and turn around to glance at her.

"You're crying."

His voice, stunned and disbelieving, reached her through the bleak void that engulfed her. She opened her eyes. He was staring at her in the oddest way. She touched her fingers to her left cheek and was amazed to feel tears. She hadn't even realized that they'd slipped from between her lashes. But they had, and there were more, sliding silently down her face.

"Ugh! I hate crying," she exclaimed shakily, and

jumped to her feet in search of a tissue. She found one and hastily wiped her eyes, struggling for control. "It doesn't do any good. It feels terrible when you're doing it, and makes you feel even worse afterward."

Nick seemed transfixed by the sight of her tears. "I've never seen you cry," he said softly. "Never, not once in all the years I've known you. And God only knows you've had plenty to cry over."

"I have no use for silly, emotional tears," Candy said sternly, more to herself than to him.

He slowly walked toward her. "Candy," he said tentatively.

She slowly, steadily backed away from him. "I don't know what's the matter with me. For the past few months my emotions have been too close to the surface and I—I—" She broke off, aware that she was revealing too much. She flushed, embarrassed by her loss of composure.

"You've always been the most controlled—and controlling—person I've ever met," Nick said. "Maybe you're finally beginning to break loose from that stranglehold you've kept on yourself all these years."

"Or maybe I'm finally cracking up," she said in a dark attempt at humor. She attempted a strategic side step around the coffee table and missed. She would have stumbled backward if Nick hadn't been there to grab her.

Which he did, his big hands fastening around her wrists. Slowly, inexorably, he drew her toward him. "Why did you lead me to believe that you were Victoria's natural mother?" he asked softly, his onyx gaze burning into hers.

"Not for revenge," she murmured.

"Then why, Candy?"

Her heart seemed to stop beating. He was so close to her—close enough for her to feel the heat emanating from his hard, masculine frame; close enough for her to inhale the clean, woodsy scent of his after-shave.

The aroma awakened a thousand sensual memories, which washed over her in a languorous wave.

"Nick." His name escaped from her throat in a husky whisper, and she tried to move closer. She wanted to touch him with an urgency that made her ache. Desire, as sharp as a stiletto, sliced through her. She wanted to lose herself in his arms, she acknowledged, to feel his hot, hard mouth take hers. Her eyes held his and she gazed at him with undisguised yearning.

But Nick didn't let her close the inches-wide gap between them. He was holding her wrists, controlling her movements to keep her anchored firmly in place. "Tell me, Candace." His voice was deep and low.

Hunger and need rippled through her, intensified by the sensual frustration he was inducing by holding her away from him. She wanted to wrap her arms around him and melt into his hard, masculine strength. A hot spear of sexual excitement rendered her breathless. A delicious feminine need to submit to his powerful virility crept inexorably through her. She began to tremble. Her body was conditioned to the pleasure and fulfillment she had known with Nick. It was always like this with him, she thought dizzily. Only with him.

Still not allowing her to touch him, he bent his head and brushed her lips with his. The brief contact electrified her. Her knees went weak, and her lashes fluttered shut.

"Why, Candy?"

She moaned. "You ask too many questions, Nick. Please drop it. And please, please . . ." She paused, shuddering, and gasped for breath. She was begging him, pleading for him, but she didn't care. She didn't care about anything but the fierce, sweet agony of belonging to him again.

Nick stared at her. God, she was beautiful, he thought as a fierce rush of desire surged through him. Wouldn't he ever stop wanting her? He gazed down at her smooth, milky skin, at her exquisitely shaped mouth with her lips sweetly parted. Her breasts, rounded and full, rose and fell softly as her breathing quickened. He knew what they looked like bare, soft and warm and white, tipped by dusky pink nipples. He wanted to touch them, to taste them. He wanted her with an intensity that almost stopped his heart.

"Stop talking and kiss you, is that what you mean?" he asked in a raspy voice. "Stop talking and make love to you?"

She slipped her slim calf between his and rubbed sensuously against the cool cloth of his trousers. "Yes, Nick, yes. Oh, Nick, I've missed you so much. I—"

He abruptly released her and stepped away. Candy's eyes flew open. "Nick?" she whispered huskily, reaching for him.

"If I kiss you, we'll be in bed within fifteen minutes," he said flatly. "No, ten. And we won't even make it to the bedroom. I want to be inside you so badly, I'll lay you down on the sofa and take you right here and now."

She moved toward him. "That's what I want, too, Nick."

It was his turn to retreat from her. "It's wrong, Candy," he said roughly, "You, me. This whole scene is all wrong for us both."

"No," she protested, shaking her head vigorously. "It's right, Nick. We've always been right together."

But to her dismay, he didn't take her back into his arms. Instead, he folded his arms across his chest and gazed at her with an unnerving scrutiny. "I never thought I'd hear those words from you, Candy. Not after all the years of listening to you insist that our relationship was an unhealthy addiction that we needed to break. Well, you finally convinced me, honey. I refuse to be hooked on you any longer. I'm not getting involved with you again. Not sexually involved. Not emotionally involved. Not involved, period."

His words hurt. But Candy had had a lifetime of coping with hurt, and she wasn't about to start falling apart now. Her old protective reflexes kicked in. When in pain, get mad. Strike back and get even. "It didn't look that way a few seconds ago," she said, taunting him. "You damn well were sexually involved with me. And emotionally involved too. Stop kidding yourself and admit it, Nick."

A mirthless smile curved his lips. "All right, I admit that you can still get to me. But I'm on my way to recovery, Candace. Do you realize that this is the first time I've ever been able to call a halt to our lovemaking?"

"You don't have to sound so proud of yourself," Candy snapped. She felt tears welling up again and was aghast. She would *not* cry over him—in front of him yet!—twice in the same night. Not when he was gloating about successfully rejecting her!

"Oh, go home, Nick. I don't want you any way." Her voice rose in sharp, defensive anger. "In fact, I'm thrilled to be rid of you. You're domineering and aggressive and intrusive and—"

"The only man who's ever been able to stand up to you," he said, interrupting. "The only man you've never managed to break into pieces, although God knows you've come close on more than one occasion."

And she'd do it again if he were to drop his guard and take up with her; he was sure of it. But that didn't stop him from wanting her. Wanting her desperately. Despite all his fervid disavowals, he knew damn well that she still had him in sexual chains. She had to know it too. Rebellion surged within him.

"I've had it!" he growled. "This tangled, torturous relationship of ours is impossible. You can't know how much I heartily regret the time I helped you open your damn locker that first day of sophomore year at Hoover High." That fateful day had been the start of it all. She had smiled at him, and he'd been lost.

Candy gave her dark hair a toss. "I remember that day very well. You nearly tripped over your own feet rushing across the hall to help me. And then you carried my books and walked me to Kramer's Drugstore after school and bought me a cherry cola. You were mad about me, the whole class knew it."

"Yeah, they did." Nick shook his head ruefully. "And your own twin brother tried to warn me against you. I should have listened to him. 'Keep away from Candy,' he said. 'She has a terrible temper and she doesn't put out.' "

"That sounds like something Case would say," Candy exclaimed indignantly.

"Well, he was right about your temper, but wrong about your putting out." A sudden, wicked grin crossed his face. "You did eventually. Remember the night of our senior prom?"

A soft smile played at the corners of her mouth. "The night you finally got around to deflowering me? Yes, Nick, I remember. I'll never forget it."

"*Finally* got around to deflowering you?" Nick repeated with mock indignation. "Baby, I kept diligently trying to deflower you from the day we met, but you kept holding out. We made history at Hoover High—we were the only couple ever to go together that long without going all the way. Some of our classmates were parents before you got around to letting me take off your bra."

"Poor Nick," Candy said softly, tauntingly. "I remember the captain of the football team telling me quite seriously that I was depriving you and that it was affecting your performance on the field. He suggested I 'give it to you' for the sake of Hoover High's standing in the city football league."

"The captain of the football team, good old Jack Kozimer," Nick said with a fondly reminiscent grin. "He married Linda Maloney a year after graduation and went through two tours in 'Nam and won two Purple Hearts. Jack and Linda are still in Detroit. He's an assembly-line foreman for Ford. They have three kids."

"I know. I spent a long time reminiscing about our old school days with Linda at our last high-school reunion," Candy said with a smile. "We talked about phys-ed class and our narcoleptic gym teacher, selling Cokes at the football games, dancing to that great Motown music at the Friday night dances . . . Oh, Nick, remember the Isley Brothers and our favorite songs, 'Shout' and 'This Old Heart of Mine Is Weak for You'?"

Nick nodded, smiling. "Remember the senior class talent show when you and Linda and Diane Pecoraro put on those incredible wigs and lip-synched to the Supremes?" he recalled, getting caught up in the nostalgic spirit.

"And then you and Case and Jack Kozimer and Tony Jackson worked up that crazy routine for your lip-synch of the Four Tops." Candy laughed. "We were so mad that you guys stole our idea—and then had the nerve to win first prize!"

Nick joined in her laughter. "They called us back out onstage for an encore performance. I can still remember some of the steps—and all of the words to our song, 'I Can't Help Myself.'" He scowled suddenly as the lyrics flashed through his head: "A fool in love." He certainly had been.

"I didn't know I'd end up living the lyrics," he said grimly. Their brief truce was over. They were back to being romantic adversaries again. "It's as if they were written especially for our arduous romance."

"I used to wonder if we'd ever be free of each other," Candy murmured. "But maybe we've never really wanted to be." She lifted her gaze to his.

"If that's an invitation, our timing is off, as usual," Nick said gruffly. "I'm determined to be free of you at last, Candy. To conjure up a somewhat aquatic metaphor, there's just been too much water over the dam."

She said nothing. His words hurt too much, and this time she couldn't seem to summon the fiery anger that she always managed to substitute for pain.

The silence between them was tense. Candy stared blindly at the flickering images on the television screen.

Nick idly picked up one of the framed photographs sitting on the end table and stared at it.

Candy took a step closer to him and glanced at the photo he held. "That's Case and his wife, Sharla," she said, her voice thick with the hurt that her pride wouldn't let her express. "I think I told you that he's a trauma surgeon at the Hospital Center in D.C. Sharla is a pediatric specialist there, one of the best. The little girl in the picture is their daughter Shannon. She's fourteen months old, just the same age as your Nichole."

"She's a cute little thing," Nick remarked. "Dark eyes, dark hair. The spitting image of her mother, but I see a little of Case in her too." He picked up a family photograph of the Wickwires and stared at the pictures of both families. "I'd forgotten that Case and Shay both have those same striking blue eyes. You always used to lament not having the 'Flynn eyes,' as you called them."

"And you would always tell me that you liked my green eyes better, anyway," Candy reminded him softly.

"I've always thought that you had the most beautiful eyes I'd ever seen." His voice lowered. "I still do." And then he caught himself. This was *not* the way to disengage himself from her. He determinedly dropped the topic of her beautiful green eyes and moved to a safer subject. "It looks like both of Shay's kids have those Flynn blue eyes, though," he said a bit too heartily.

"Tori has them too. She—" Candy abruptly lapsed into an appalled silence. His revealing compliment had so delighted her that she'd dropped her guard and consequently blurted out what she'd never meant to say. Nick Torchia was the only person in the world who had that effect on her, she silently lamented. She prayed that he wouldn't pick up on her slip.

He did, of course. He never missed a thing, particularly if it pertained to her. He picked up a picture of Tori, taken the month before, and studied it intently. "Those big, wide-set eyes," he said thoughtfully. "That distinctive piercing blue color. Tori is a Flynn, not only by adoption but by birth, as well, isn't she?"

"Don't be absurd!" Candy snapped. "Millions of people in the world have blue eyes. *Millions*! Just because Tori happens to—"

"You're trembling," Nick observed, and reached for her wrist. His strong fingers located her pulse point. "And your pulse is racing. You're as nervous as I've ever seen you, Candace."

"Leave me alone!" She jerked her arm away. "I refuse to discuss your insane speculations. It's time for you to leave, Nick. Now."

He refused to move. "When the frighteningly self-possessed Candace Flynn loses her cool, the investigator in me comes immediately to the fore. I'm beginning to put together some pieces of the puzzle. Why you decided it would be easier if I thought you were Tori's natural mother, for one. You didn't want me to guess at her real parentage."

"Are you having fun playing Sherlock Holmes?" Candy countered crossly.

He ignored her jibe. "Tori was born a Flynn, and you claim that you didn't give birth to her. I believe you. You wouldn't lie about that. Obviously Shay didn't have her. That leaves your brother, Case. He's Tori's father, isn't he, Candy?"

"No!" cried Candy, aghast. "Don't you dare say such a thing! Case is a happily married man. He adores his wife! They're devoted to each other and to their little girl."

"But Case had an affair, and little Tori is the result of his lapse in fidelity. You knew his marriage would be threatened, so you took it upon yourself to handle the situation. You paid off the mother, adopted the baby, and no one is the wiser, especially not Case's wife."

"I won't even dignify that absurd piece of fiction with a response!" spluttered Candy.

"I don't expect you to. You've always been loyal to a fault to your brother and sister, Candy." He'd always admired her intense loyalty to her siblings—and had always wished that she would extend it to include him too. "Naturally you'd do anything to help Case save his marriage."

"Nick, you're wrong," Candy said urgently.

Nick continued to stare at the pictures. "No, I'm not. It's as plain as the color in these photos. Case, Shay, Scotty, Brandon, and Tori—there's a resemblance between them all. Don't try to tell me that they aren't related by blood. And to you, Candy."

"I—I won't, but it's not the way you think." Candy balled her fingers into fists. She was desperate now. "Tori isn't Case's child, Nick, she's his niece. And mine. You see, there is another Flynn you don't know about, and who Case and Shay don't know about, either. She's our half sister, born during our father's second marriage. Her name is Angelynne, and she's nineteen years old. I first met her when she was just an infant, only a few months old. Angelynne gave birth to Tori and then gave her to me."

"What? For Pete's sake, Candy, this sounds like one of those convoluted soap-opera plots where long-lost relatives appear on the doorstep from out of the blue. You've never mentioned a very young half sister to me before, and you've been closer to me than to anyone else."

"I've never told a soul about Angelynne, Nick. Not even Case or Shay. But she exists, and she's the one who had Tori." Candy walked over to a magazine rack and pulled out a copy of *People* magazine. She quickly flipped to an article and showed him the page. "That's Angelynne," she said, her tone laced with a mixture of pride and defiance.

Nick stared at the photograph of an exotic, dark-haired, blue-eyed beauty, sitting on the shoulders of a well-known rock star and laughing into the camera. " 'Actress/model Angelynne Flynn is riding high these days,' " he read. He looked up at Candy, his expression revealing his surprise.

"Angelynne is very talented," said Candy, gazing at the picture. "She's been in New York just five months and has already been cast as Kimberly, the teenage heroine in a daytime soap opera. She's done a commercial for suntan lotion and posed for a blue jeans ad too. She works very hard, taping the soap in the mornings and taking acting and dancing classes a couple of times a week."

"I can hardly take it in." Nick's eyes kept returning to the photograph. "You mean, Shay has had this magazine in her house with a picture of her own sister in it, and she's completely unaware of the relationship? And Case knows absolutely nothing of this other sister, either? Neither knows that little Tori is really a blood relative to all of you?"

"I know it seems strange, but it's true."

"Strange isn't the half of it! Try bizarre! How—*why*—did you keep this younger half sister a secret all these years, Candy?"

"Nick, it's a long story. . . ."

He sat down on the sofa. "I'm ready to hear it, Candy."

"I just don't know if I'm ready to tell it."

His arm snaked out to capture her hand, and he tugged her down beside him. "You can start by telling me why you kept this girl a secret from your own sister and brother, who also happen to be *her* own sister and brother."

He wasn't going to let her get out of it, Candy acknowledged with a sigh. Nick could be as tenacious and stubborn as she could. Yet, inexplicably, in some small corner of her mind she was relieved that he'd found out. Part of her actually *wanted* to share her secret with him, she realized in surprise. Or at least some of the secret.

"At first I thought it was for the best not to mention Angelynne's existence," she began hesitantly. "I was an emotional wreck the day that my father arrived at my apartment with his new wife, Rainelle, and their baby, Angelynne." She stared absently into space. "It was the year you'd been sent to Vietnam, Nick. The year that I lost our . . . our baby."

Nick glanced at her sharply, astonished that she'd referred to that traumatic time. He knew how assiduously she avoided mentioning it. "That was the worst year of my life," he said quietly. "You needed me and I couldn't be with you. And after the way we'd parted—"

Candy looked away. "Telling Case and Shay about Dad's new family seemed more than I could cope with at the time. You know how much Case has always despised Dad, and Shay was still a kid, but she hated Dad too. I knew they'd be hostile at the mere mention of anyone or anything connected to him. It seemed so much easier just to give Dad the money he asked for and send them on their way."

"But you obviously kept in contact with them," Nick prompted.

She nodded solemnly. "I felt sorry for Rainelle. She was a born victim, if there ever was one. I knew her life with my father would be hell, and I especially felt sorry for pretty little Angelynne. There was something about that baby . . ." She closed her eyes, remembering.

"She reminded you of the child you lost?" Nick suggested softly.

"Maybe," Candy whispered. "Although I never knew if it was a boy or a girl. The doctor said it was too early to know."

"Do you realize that this is the closest we've ever come to talking about your miscarriage?" Nick impulsively covered one of her hands with his own. "Candy, there is so much that I've wanted to—"

"I thought you wanted to hear about Angelynne," Candy said, setting her jaw with a determination he knew well. She removed her hand from beneath his.

Nick sighed in frustration. He knew how completely she withdrew when emotionally pressured. Once again the words would remain unsaid. "I do. Please continue, Candy."

"Well, not surprisingly, Dad left his new family for parts unknown before Angelynne was two years old," said Candy. "Rainelle was desperate, and she called me in hysterics."

"She needed money, and once again it was Candy to the rescue," surmised Nick.

"I started sending Rainelle money every month for Angelynne. Small amounts at first, but I increased the sum after I got out of law school and established my law practice. I made it a point to visit Angelynne several times a year. She was a very bright and headstrong child, and by the time she was twelve, she was more than poor Rainelle could handle. Plus, Rainelle had such atrocious taste in men. I was terrified that one of them might . . . would"—she paused—"bother Angelynne. I wanted to get her away before something happened, so I arranged for her to attend a boarding school near here. She did very well there. I saw her every other weekend until she graduated. I arranged for her mother to come for holidays, and they spent them together."

"And all the while you kept her existence a secret," Nick said, still reeling over the disclosure. Being Candy, she would have figured it was her responsibility to handle everything on her own. She was evasive and carefully compartmentalized the emotions, events, and people in her life. "Your whole life is a series of secrets," he added, frowning. "You've never even told Case or Shay that our relationship survived high school." And he knew she would never, ever mention to anyone that she'd briefly carried—and lost—their child.

Who would no longer be a child today, he realized with a start. Once again his gaze strayed to the magazine photograph. Their child, had it lived to be born, would be a nineteen-year-old, like Angelynne. He tried to imagine what his feelings would be if his sweet little Nichole were to perch astride a seedy musician's shoulders at some future date. Or to give birth to an out-of-wedlock child.

The images unnerved him. For the first time since Nicki's birth, he wondered if he really could cope with the ups and downs of parenthood all by himself. He glanced up, and his dark eyes collided with Candy's pensive green ones. He wondered if she harbored any such doubts about single parenthood and knew she wouldn't tell him if she did. The silence stretched between them.

"And now you've taken on Tori," he said at last. "How did that come about?"

Candy sighed. "After Angelynne graduated, she headed straight to California. She was determined to have an acting career. Unfortunately she fell madly in love with a boy in one of her acting classes out there. He wasn't serious about her, and when he broke up with her, she didn't tell him she was pregnant. She never told me, either. She kept making excuses about why I couldn't visit her. And then she turned up with Tori, who was just four days old." Her voice was taut with emotion. "I wanted the baby from the moment I saw her, and Angelynne wanted me to have her."

"So you adopted Tori and sent Angelynne to New York." Nick grimaced. "Candy, that's the most unbelievable story I've ever heard. Straight out of that soap Angelynne's starring in."

"You won't tell anyone, will you, Nick?" Candy pressed urgently. "Please promise me that you won't."

"Candy, why all the secrets?" He stared at her, his exasperation evident in his expression and even more so in his tone. "There's no need for it, at least not anymore. Case and Shay are adults, and they're certainly capable of coping with the existence of Angelynne. I'll go with you to explain things to them, if you'd like. They—"

"No!" Candy said, interrupting quickly. "Please, Nick, let me handle things my way. Promise me that you'll never breathe a word of any of this to anybody."

Nick scowled. "Do you know how much I hate being dragged into your totally unnecessary web of secrecy and conspiracy? It's crazy." His frustration grew, fueled by the futility of it all. "For years we had an on-again, off-again relationship that nobody was allowed to know about. You were pregnant with my child, but we—"

Candy abruptly stood up. "Nick, I won't listen to this!" *I can't* listen, she added silently. She'd long feared that if she were ever to open the floodgates, she would never be able to get hold of herself again. The prospect of herself breaking apart like that was terrifying; she didn't dare take such a risk, especially now, with a helpless child depending on her.

It seemed as if there was always a helpless child depending on her to stay strong, she mused thoughtfully. Currently it was Tori, but Angelynne and Shay had preceded her.

Nick didn't know that, of course. He thought she was stubborn, evasive, and controlling. Which, Candy conceded with an inward sigh, she was, whatever her motives.

They were at yet another impasse. Nick felt his exasperation and frustration meld into fresh, cold anger.

"There you go again," he said tightly. "You'll never be completely open, will you, Candy? I don't think you're capable of it. You let me come so close, and then—bam! The walls go up."

"You'd prefer me to cry all over you, I suppose? To come running to you to solve all my problems? Well, I'm not a weeper or a whiner, Nick. I don't fall apart, I get things done. And you, like every other man I've ever met, resent me for it."

"You always manage to miss the point completely," Nick marveled, shaking his head. "I admire your strength, Candace, I always have. But I also value openness and honesty, and I'm afraid those very concepts are incomprehensible to you."

A fierce desolation washed over her. Maybe they were. "Too much water over the dam," he'd said. Well, maybe he was right. She fought against the chill feeling of hopelessness that enveloped her. It reminded her of the dark, hopeless days of her childhood when she'd been small and helpless and totally at the mercy of the whims of undependable, unpredictable adults. Not anymore, she thought, consoling herself. *She* was the adult now, and she'd made it a point to be totally dependable and rigidly predictable. No one was ever going to make her feel hopeless and helpless again.

"I don't need you to judge me," she said icily. "And I don't need you to interfere in my life or my family. It's definitely time for you to go, Nick."

As always, she looked beautiful in her anger, her eyes flashing emerald fire, her cheeks flushed a delicate pink. Nick felt his anger and frustration abruptly turn physical as a hard shaft of desire stabbed him.

Why couldn't she look like some kind of freaking hag when she lost her temper? he wondered with an inward groan. His loins tightened. She was beautiful, passionate, desirable. She was Candy, the woman he'd loved for so long, he could hardly remember a time when he hadn't loved her.

And he'd already wasted too many years wanting what he never could have with her, he reminded himself fiercely.

"I agree. I shouldn't have come in the first place." He rose to his feet, fighting the urge to pull her against him, to satisfy the burning, primitive hunger she always managed to evoke within him. No matter how angry or exasperated he felt with her, he couldn't control his physical response to her. He fought the image forming in his mind, tormenting and tempting him: the image of Candy lying naked beneath him, whimpering those hot little cries of passion as he moved in and out of her.

With some difficulty he walked from the room. Fortunately Candy was behind him and couldn't see the indisputable evidence of the effect she was having on him.

"And don't bother to try to see me again," she flung after him. She wanted to push him away as much as she wanted him to stay. Her ambivalence and confusion enraged her.

He gave a short laugh. "Honey, you have no worries there." It had been a major mistake even to speak to her at the baby shop, he thought as he climbed the stairs. He felt turned inside out by these few short hours they'd spent together.

She stood in the hall and watched as he silently carried his sleeping baby daughter down the stairs. It hurt to swallow around the lump that had lodged in her throat. She hadn't wanted the evening to end in animosity. Some part of her knew that Nick was her ally, not her adversary. Why—why did she always drive him away?

Nick carried the sleeping Nichole to his car, a wine-red Buick Riviera, which was parked in front of the house. Candy followed, watching silently, numbly, as he strapped the baby into the safety seat.

"Candy," Nick called softly, seconds before he climbed behind the wheel of the car. "I won't tell anyone about Angelynne or Tori. I owe you that much."

Candy said nothing. Yet another of her secrets was safe with him, she thought bleakly as she watched him drive away. But at what cost?

There was no use moping about it. Nick didn't want to rekindle the flame between them, she told herself bracingly. And neither should she, because Nick, who so valued openness and honesty, would be positively apoplectic if he were to learn that she was keeping yet another secret. One involving him.

Candy shivered. How outraged Nick would be if he ever found *that* out! And he would have every right to be, she conceded.

She stared silently into the night sky. Nick's passion for honesty and openness, combined with his ability to decipher the facts, posed definite problems for her, for all of them. She should be glad that he was so determined to be out of her life forever. She *was* glad, she told herself with characteristic Candy Flynn ferocity.

Squaring her shoulders, she walked resolutely back into the house and waited for news of Shay.

Her brother-in-law's call came a short while later. She had a brand-new niece, Adam jubilantly informed her. Elizabeth Candace Wickwire weighed in at seven pounds and was beautiful, with dark hair and those big, Flynn blue eyes. Both mother and child were fine.

Candy was elated. Her first impulse was to share the good news with Nick, but she instantly squelched it. They'd just parted forever. Again. If she called him, he would accuse her of playing games. Again. She would lash out at him. Again. She sighed.

If Nick only knew how often she thought of him, despite the years and distance that had separated them. If he only knew how she ached for him.

But how could she tell him when he'd stated expressly that he wanted nothing more to do with her? She'd spent her childhood trying to give love to parents who didn't want it, and she wasn't about to repeat that mistake with a man who didn't want her. She'd learned not to take emotional risks. She'd learned how to face facts too. Nick Torchia was out of her life forever.

Four

The Markham divorce was a bitter, contested one. Candy viewed the warring spouses and their respective attorneys from her position on the bench and tried to force herself to remain neutral.

It wasn't easy. She continually had to fight against her natural inclination to ally herself with one side or the other. Once again she found herself doubting her proficiency as a judge. Originally she had viewed her appointment as the ultimate career advancement. She'd accepted her elevation to the bench without a qualm as to whether it was right for her. Or if she was right for it.

Everyone else—her family, friends, and colleagues—had shared her enthusiasm for her new position. Only Nick had questioned it. "I don't think you'll be happy as a judge," he'd said bluntly. "Think about it, Candy. A judge has no battles to fight, no fights to win, and that's what you thrive on. You're a premier divorce lawyer; your prowess is legendary in this area. You should keep on doing what you're doing and leave the judging to others."

She hadn't appreciated his frankness. In fact, she'd exploded and accused him of being a sexist pig who didn't want to see women in positions of authority.

She'd wanted his approval and affirmation and had been hurt when he didn't offer it, so she'd attacked him as ferociously as a rat when cornered, Candy acknowledged gloomily. They'd had one of their worst fights, followed by a bitter parting. Six months later he had arrived at the high-school reunion with Sherrie.

Candy stifled a groan. It was hard to admit to herself that Nick had been right. Her dissatisfaction as a judge had begun when she'd heard her first case and had continued to mount ever since.

Her methods as a "bomber/barracuda" divorce lawyer had been unfailing. Developing a strong allegiance to each of her clients, she was thorough, aggressive, and intense, actively seeking to win each case and using all of her considerable energy and legal talent to do so. Her personality had been perfectly tailored to her skills, a fact that Nick had pointed out. A fact that she had chosen to ignore.

She'd never dreamed how different it would be, Candy thought as she listened to one of the attorneys drone on. A judge had to be—well, nonjudgmental during a trial. A judge was essentially passive, sitting calmly and listening, weighing the facts, remaining objective and almost uninvolved until the end, when it came time to render the verdict.

As Nick had predicted, the very qualities that had made her an unsurpassed divorce attorney worked against her as a judge. The truth was that she'd made a mistake—a big one—in giving up her law practice. She remembered how obsessed she'd always been with grades—from elementary school through law school. Well, grade-wise, her performances and abilities as a lawyer rated a stellar $A+$. As a judge, she passed with a mere C.

Her gaze flickered from one of the Markhams to the other. The divorcing couple were glaring at each other from opposite sides of the courtroom. The husband was small in stature and had a short, ridiculous black mustache that gave him a startling resemblance to

Adolf Hitler. Candy disliked him and his attorney, who managed to be both supercilious and incompetent at the same time. The opposing side wasn't much better. The wife appeared to have the temperament of a pitbull. Her attorney was prissy and self-righteous and seemed to speak in italics, dramatically enunciating each word.

A judge couldn't choose her cases like an attorney could choose her clients—which was another difficult aspect of being on the bench, Candy thought, even as she reprimanded herself for her unjuristlike thoughts. If she were still practicing law, she would have refused to represent both the Hitler clone and his snarling, soon-to-be ex-wife. If she were still practicing law, she would have demolished both of these plodding and uninspired attorneys in the opening argument. If . . .

Candy forced her runaway thoughts back to the business at hand. One did not live a life by playing the what-if game. She *was* the judge, and she had to render a fair and impartial decision. And then she could go home to Tori. Her lips curved into a soft smile at the thought of the baby. She might be plagued by career uncertainties, but she'd never had a moment's doubt about the rightness of taking Angelynne's child to raise as her own.

Mrs. Markham's sudden, piercing scream abruptly jarred Candy's attention back to the courtroom drama now unfolding before her. Mr. Markham jumped to his feet and hurled a string of invectives at his shrieking spouse. Mrs. Markham took a swing at him and missed but sent his attorney's glasses flying across the courtroom. Mr. M. tried to hit his wife over the head with a briefcase, but she whacked him in the face with her large purse first. Candy reached for her gavel and thumped it with all her might, but commotion reigned until two bailiffs rushed into the courtroom and physically separated the battling Markhams.

The courtroom fracas was the subject at lunch later that day. Candy shared a table with Roger Wright and Jack Benton, two of her fellow family-court judges.

"The bailiff told me that the couple was totally out of control," Judge Wright remarked as he reached for the bottle of ketchup. "He's convinced that if either of them had had a gun, they would have shot up the courtroom."

"That sort of thing has become too common these days. I'd like to see bulletproof shields in the courtrooms and hearing rooms," said Judge Benton with a nervous grimace. "And metal detectors and closed-circuit monitors in the hallways and anterooms outside the judges' chambers."

Wright nodded. "Tony Tesone has asked for bids on the security work. He told me he was particularly impressed with the firm you recommended, Candy. Apparently they've done security work for a number of courtrooms in California and have a whole list of glowing recommendations."

"TSI—Torch Security Incorporated." Candy said the name with a touch of vicarious pride. When Court Administrator Tesone had discussed the necessity for courtroom security measures with the family-court judges two weeks ago, she had been delighted to have the opportunity to recommend Nick's firm—even if he had made no attempt to contact her during the past two weeks; even if she had waited every night hoping he'd call, like a lovesick high-school girl with a hopeless crush; even if she had to give herself bracing pep talks at least five times a day on why she was glad Nick Torchia was forever out of her life.

"Well, I hope Tesone hires the best, regardless of cost, and they implement the security measures pronto," said Judge Benton, frowning at his tuna melt. "We don't want a repeat of that incident in Florida around here."

The other two nodded solemnly, recalling the notorious alimony hearing where the judge, an attorney, and a witness had been shot to death by a gun-toting defendant.

"And everything should be in place before this Baby Jay fiasco begins," Benton added testily. "Lord only knows

how many lunatics will be drawn by all the publicity."
He cast Roger Wright a severe look. "I've made it clear
that I'm not interested in hearing that case, haven't
I?"

Judge Wright smiled wryly. "You've made it extremely
clear, Jack. You disqualify yourself from it at least once
a day."

"Well, I mean it." Benton scowled. "A mess like that
surely would put me back in the hospital for surgery
on my ulcer. Assign the case to Candace here. She's a
single woman with a child. Who better to hear a custody case between three single women? Every feminist
group in the country will stand up and cheer if she
gets the case."

Roger murmured noncommittally. Candy concentrated
on her soup and refrained from comment. She knew
she didn't want to be assigned the case solely because
of her gender, but she had an uncomfortable feeling
that it might come to that. What a dilemma, she thought
glumly. She'd made the wrong career move and might
now be handed a career-making case for that wrong
career—and for all the wrong reasons.

Everything seemed wrong these days, she admitted
silently, feeling as disgruntled as Judge Benton looked
when he talked about his ulcer. Tori was the only
bright spot in her life, the only real and constant source
of satisfaction.

If only Nick— She fiercely squelched that thought.
No, she thought, scolding herself sternly. *If only* and
what if were two strictly forbidden phrases, not to be
used by Candace Flynn. She refused to want a man
who didn't want her; she did *not* need Nick Torchia in
her life.

"There's Tony Tesone now," said Judge Benton. "Let's
ask him for the latest on the security situation." He
motioned the court administrator over to the table before Candy had a chance to see that Tesone was not
alone.

He was accompanied by Nick Torchia.

The slate-gray suit he wore was as conservative as any well-heeled banker's, yet seemed to heighten his aura of masculine toughness. Nick looked like a man who could cope with violence and invariably emerge the victor. Even the ever anxious Judge Benton brightened when the introductions were made and he was told that TSI had won the security consulting bid and would begin work on the project immediately.

"You know, family court is the most volatile court in the system. A number of our litigants are downright wild," Benton advised Nick gravely. "The civil division is far more dignified. In the criminal courts they have good security. But in the family division, where cases are more emotional than in any other, we've had a greater number of threats and attacks than any other court. Fortunately there hasn't been a life-endangering threat yet, but I've often felt that it's just a matter of time."

Nick patiently launched into an explanation of his plans for courtroom security, right down to the bullet-proof shields that would protect the judges as they sat on the bench and could withstand bullets from a .357 Magnum or a 9-mm automatic.

And all the while he was talking, he kept stealing glances at Candy. She was wearing a trim business suit, the color of cocoa, with a cream-colored silk blouse, and her dark hair was pulled back into a properly conservative twist. Her makeup and attire were impeccable and thoroughly appropriate for her elevated position. She was certainly not projecting a sexually provocative image, yet his reaction to her was the same as it would be if she were wearing a diaphanous negligee and her hair were tousled sexily around her shoulders. He wanted her. He was growing hard, and the fullness created a strain against his clothing. Grabbing a chair from a nearby table, he pulled it over and sat down between the two men, directly across from Candy.

She looked up and their eyes met. She swallowed, her lips parting involuntarily as she tried to gulp more air.

His dark, dark eyes held a message that she immediately recognized, one she knew well. Unconsciously running the tip of her tongue over her lips, she sent him a message of her own.

For that moment, the court administrator and the other two judges might as well have disappeared, so intense was Nick and Candy's absorption in each other. But the garrulous Judge Benton swiftly reasserted himself into the private, sensual spell that bound the couple—and abruptly broke it.

Benton launched into a gruesome tale—he seemed to possess a never-ending supply—of yet another courtroom bloodbath, and Nick responded with a catalog of devices and procedures his firm would use to guarantee the personal safety of courtroom personnel. Candy listened, impressed with Nick's calm competence as he spoke, an expert in his field.

His voice, deep, with a rough, masculine edge to it, had never failed to arouse her. It was arousing her now, even though he was speaking of such prosaic things as Armortex shields. She felt flushed with heat, her nerves wound like a spring. Her breasts swelled against the cool beige silk of her camisole, and her nipples tingled and tightened. There was an aching, pulsing warmth deep, deep within her. Compulsively her eyes kept returning to Nick, but he was assiduously avoiding even glancing in her direction.

To an observer it would appear that Nick Torchia was thoroughly absorbed in his discussion of security measures with the judges and the court administrator. Only he knew that he was operating on automatic pilot—he could give this security speech in his sleep—and his mind was wholly, completely occupied with Candy's presence.

He tried to steel himself against her and the feelings she so effortlessly evoked in him. He'd purposely avoided any contact with her at all these past two weeks. He was *not* going to get involved with her again, no matter how great the temptation, Nick reminded himself firmly.

He was seeking moderation and balance in his life, and this unshakable obsession he seemed to have for Candace Flynn just wasn't part of his plans. Somehow he was going to shake it, he vowed. He was!

"Excuse me, I have an appointment. I'm going to have to leave now."

Candy's voice, cool and well modulated, interrupted both his security lecture and his simultaneous mental meanderings. Nick started visibly and stared at her. She had risen from her chair to address the men at the table collectively.

"Nick, I'm delighted that your firm will be doing the security work in the family-court division," she said to him, her voice briskly professional, her demeanor starchily efficient. Her gaze was focused somewhere above his head, adding to the impersonality of the exchange.

She nodded to the three other men, then exited with regal flair.

"You say she's an old friend of yours?" Judge Wright asked Nick, his voice holding a note of disbelief.

And no wonder, thought Nick. Candy certainly hadn't displayed the slightest hint of friendliness toward him. Aside from a brief nod when he first joined them, she'd scarcely acknowledged his presence. Even her polite parting words had sounded frostily perfunctory.

"We've known each other since high school," Nick replied carefully. "We've kept in touch throughout the years."

A major understatement there, he thought wryly, self-mockingly. But if the others hadn't seen past the remote attitude she'd projected toward him, Nick had. He'd seen her eyes darken when they met and hold his for that one unguarded moment. He'd seen her breathing quicken, and he'd known . . . he'd known.

"And then there was the case of the sniper who holed up in a hearing room in a courthouse out in Indiana." Judge Benton's voice boomed, and Nick jerked forward. "What sort of protection does your firm offer against a threat like that, Nick?"

Taking a deep, sharp breath, Nick thrust Candy from his mind and proceeded to answer the question.

Nichole had had a very short nap that afternoon, and consequently she fell asleep in her father's arms soon after her dinner. Nick glanced at his watch. Six-thirty. The evening loomed ahead of him. He had a date at nine and had intended to fill the early-evening hours playing with the baby. Who'd conked out on him. He jostled her a little, hoping to wake her, feeling slightly guilty about it. But Nichole stayed peacefully asleep.

He sighed and carried her upstairs to her crib. "Maybe I should wake her for a bath?" he hopefully asked Lillian, the baby's nanny.

Lillian, a practical grandmother of four, looked at him as if he were crazy. "There is no reason to awaken a sleeping baby for that," she said firmly. "I'll give Nicki a bath in the morning." She seemed to sense that he was at loose ends. "You mentioned that you were going out tonight, Nick. Why not leave early? I guarantee that Nicki isn't going to wake up. Not after the long time we spent in the park and her short nap this afternoon. She's out for the night."

Nick considered it. An idea rooted itself in his mind and refused to be dislodged. "Well, I suppose I could drop in on an—an old friend of mine before my date at nine. A sort of a business-related courtesy call. A thanks-for-the-recommendation-which-resulted-in-a-job kind of visit."

"Fine," said Lillian absently, heading toward her room. She did not seem to be particularly interested in where he was going or why. Nick was aware that he was explaining his reasons for calling on Candace Flynn more to himself than to Nichole's nanny.

But he did owe Candy something more personal than the standard thank-you card his firm routinely mailed to those who referred TSI to new customers, he assured himself. Candy *was* an old friend, and landing the courthouse job *was* a real coup for a brand-new office in the area. The least he could do was to thank her personally for the recommendation, or so he kept insisting to himself during the short drive to the nearby suburb where she lived.

By the time he swung his car in front of her two-story town house condominium, he almost had himself believing those were his reasons for being there. And when she opened the front door in response to his knock, he felt as if he'd been socked directly in the solar plexus.

The sight of her took his breath away. Her rich, dark hair swung loosely and thickly around her shoulders, and her fawn-colored light wool slacks looked as soft as her silky red blouse. The materials of both garments were temptingly sensuous, a virtual invitation to touch as they flowed over her slender figure. Her slim feet were encased in bright red leather flats. Candy wasn't a jeans–T-shirt–and sneakers type; even her casual at-home clothing was expensive, and looked it.

She subjected him to the same intense scrutiny. His dark green linen sport coat, tan slacks, and white shirt looked custom-fitted, his striped rep tie was raw silk. He looked like the powerful and successful man he'd become, light-years away from the blue-jeaned, motor-cycle-riding young tough she'd grown up with. Yet both the boy and the man would always have a special hold on her heart.

She tried to still the thoughts tumbling through her head. Nick was clearly dressed to go out. Her heart skipped a beat. Had he come here, to take *her* out?

"Hello, Nick." Her smile was politely welcoming but guarded. Her usual cool composure completely masked the powerful inward turmoil that caused her stomach to churn and her legs to turn rubbery.

Before Nick could speak, a masculine voice sounded from within. "Candy, I'm going to put on another rec-ord, okay?"

Nick froze. She was entertaining another man! The

realization hit him with the force of a steel bludgeon. Oh, he'd known there had been other men in her life through the years. He'd hated it but had had to accept the fact—after all, he'd had other women in his life too. But he'd never had to confront the intolerable spectacle of *seeing* her with another man.

And as if to add insult to injury, the music that suddenly filled the hallway was none other than the Four Tops exuberantly lamenting the trials and tribulations of trying to exorcise a lover. And being unable to do it. "I Can't Help Myself." Truly his theme song, Nick thought, disgusted with himself. Dammit, he was going to get over Candace Flynn if it was the last thing he ever did.

"I have a date tonight," he said coolly, purposefully, "but I wanted to stop by first to thank you for your recommendation to the court administrator. I'm quite pleased that TSI landed the job."

He had a date? Candy's heart sank. So now she knew what he'd been doing with himself these past two weeks—not only ignoring her but also seeing another woman! And he had the nerve to come here, to her home, and rub it in? Fury built within her. But to display anger would be to betray the horrible jealousy tearing through her. And she was not about to give Nick Torchia that satisfaction!

He'd come here to formally thank her? Fine, she'd formally respond. "Security measures in family court are long overdue," she said stiffly. "The nationwide statistics of courtroom violence have shown alarming increases during the past decade." Lord, she was beginning to sound like Judge Benton! She abruptly lapsed into silence.

The two of them glared at each other.

And then Case Flynn appeared in the hallway, a small, dark-haired, dark-eyed toddler in his arms. His jaw dropped when he saw Nick. "Torch!" he exclaimed, a smile lighting his face. "My Lord, Nick Torchia, it *is* you! It's as if that old Motown music conjured you up!

Shay mentioned that she'd seen you the day Elizabeth was born, but we had no idea how to get in touch with you."

He extended his hand for a hearty handshake, and Nick took it, smiling back at his old friend. "Case! It's wonderful to see you!" And while he expressed his delight, his mind was registering the fact that this was the man whom Candy was entertaining: her twin brother. One of his best friends from high school. His smile broadened.

"It's been so long, Case. Too long! You don't know how often I've thought of you over the years! How much I wanted to get together with you."

"Yeah, me too." Case beamed. "Guess neither of us is very good at staying in touch, huh?"

Nick's eyes flicked to Candy. Her face was impassive, but her eyes were flashing an emerald warning. Staying in touch hadn't been an option, and they both knew it. Nick couldn't have kept his relationship with Candy a secret from her brother all these years had they kept up their friendship. In a sense she had forced him to choose between their muddled romance and one of his oldest friends. A flare of resentment shot through him.

"I've kept in touch with Candy," Nick said deliberately, watching the color suffuse her cheeks. Anxiety clouded her beautiful eyes. He knew she was afraid that he was about to blurt out something about their long, complicated history. Good, he thought nastily. She deserved to be unsettled!

Not that he had any intentions of giving away any of her secrets, however. No matter how angry he was with her, he would never betray her. "At various high-school reunions," he added, watching her expel her breath in a palpable sign of relief.

Their gazes met and exchanged pointed messages. Hers, cross and accusing. His, taunting.

"But you've avoided every one of our good old Hoover High class reunions, Case." Nick turned his attention back to her brother. "We've missed our class prez. Everybody always asks about you."

Case shrugged. "Yeah, well, you know how it is. I never wanted to go back there. Not to that place, not to those times." He glanced at his sister. "I've always been amazed that Candy has."

Candy looked away. The only reason that she'd ever gone back to those class reunions was because she'd known that Nick was going to be there. And she'd ended up in bed with him after each one in a bitter-sweet reconciliation that she'd craved as much as she'd regretted—every time. Except the last one, she silently amended, that nightmare of an evening when he had arrived with Sherrie and announced his impending marriage.

Case broke the momentary silence by proudly introducing his daughter, Shannon, the bright-eyed child in his arms who hadn't stopped smiling. Nick eagerly pulled out his pictures of Nichole, and Case viewed them with the proper admiration, then insisted that Nick come in and join them. Candy pointedly didn't follow up the invitation with one of her own, but neither man paid any attention.

"Candy and I were just discussing our dear old dad," Case said, leading Nick into Candy's attractively furnished living room. On the stereo, the Supremes wailed "You Keep Me Hanging On." Again, the title seemed particularly apropos to Nick.

"You remember the inimitable Mickey Flynn, don't you, Torch?" Case asked, sitting down on the sofa with Shannon on his lap. "Our father, the family jailbird?" His voice held an unmistakable note of bitterness. "Well, he's up for parole yet again. And as sure as snow falls in Alaska, he'll show up here in Washington to hit us up for money."

"Case, I'm sure that Nick isn't interested in hearing about Dad," Candy put in swiftly.

"We don't have any secrets from Torch regarding our unvenerated father, Candy. He's been there with us, remember?" Case grimaced. "He knows all about the fighting, the drinking and gambling, the bad checks and stealing—all of it. And that was just during our high-school years! Nick, remember the time Mickey stole the money Candy had saved up for her prom dress and blew it at a crap game? Yeah, he was one helluva father. He's managed to live up to his 'reputation' every year of his life."

Candy shifted uneasily in her chair. She had discussed her father with Nick many times, and she had discussed her father with Case, of course. It was just that she'd never discussed him at the same time with Case and Nick. She wasn't sure how to integrate these two very separate parts of her life.

Case, however, had no such compunctions. "The Senior Prom, I haven't thought of that in years!" he exclaimed, casting Nick a sudden grin. "We spiked the punch, remember? And the prom queen had too much and threw up all over the principal when he tried to crown her. What a night that was!"

Yes, thought Candy, remembering. What a night. Unlike the hapless prom queen, she'd avoided the spiked punch. She hadn't needed alcohol, anyway; she'd been floating on a cloud of pure happiness, tenderly, achingly in love with Nick. And buoyed by a wild, sharp sexual excitement. She had agreed to go with him to his uncle's apartment, conveniently empty that night after the dance, and she knew that for the very first time she would not call a halt to their lovemaking.

"You and Candy doubled with me and my date that night, remember, Torch?" Case recalled. And then his smile abruptly faded. "You loaned Candy money to buy her dress after Dad stole her savings. I remember wishing that I had the money to give her, but—"

"You don't have to worry about settling an old debt at this late date, Case," Candy said acidly. "I repaid Nick for the dress the night of the prom."

Nick merely smiled, an insolent, sexy smile that made her spine tingle. If she was trying to hurt him by implying that she'd made love with him that first time to settle a debt, she had failed utterly. "Yes, she repaid me that night," he said in a drawl. "And in the most—"

"Case, I was about to get you a glass of iced tea."
Candy jumped to her feet as if scalded. She'd better
stop baiting Nick if she wanted him to keep their turbulent relationship a secret from Case. "I have some of
those macaroons that you like too. Bring Shannon into
the kitchen and we'll have some."

She purposely didn't include Nick in the invitation;
she wanted him to leave immediately. How dare he
come here, looking better than any man had a right to,
dredging up provocative old memories, *on his way to
see another woman.* But that didn't stop him from
following her and Case into her compact, modern
kitchen.

"Shannon and I are on our own this evening," Case
said to Nick, sitting down at the kitchen table. "Sharla,
my wife, has a set of preemie twins in the newborn
intensive-care unit and doesn't want to leave them until their condition stabilizes. You know, with all the
multiple births these days, people think that having
twins is risk-free, but it's really not. Sharla says . . ."
He launched into a long and complicated discourse on
the latest medical technology in the neonatology unit.

Nick tried to listen attentively, but the subject matter
was beyond him. He stole a glance at Candy. He could
tell by her expression—and her glazed eyes—that she
wasn't comprehending the medical lecture, either. He
grinned suddenly. She caught his eye but didn't smile.
She inclined her head in a display of icy hauteur.

"Hey, Candy, instead of iced tea, how about opening
a bottle of wine?" Case asked.

"I'm sure Nick can't stay, Case," she replied coolly.
"He has a date tonight. He just dropped by to thank me
for recommending his firm to the Montgomery County
court administrator."

"Oh." Case took a bite out of a macaroon and handed
his grinning baby daughter a piece of zwieback, which
she promptly began to gnaw on. "Who's your date, Nick?"

Nick cleared his throat. "Her name is Brandi How-
ard. I—uh—met her on the Metro earlier in the week."

"Brandi? And you met her on the Metro?" The sarcasm in Candy's tone was guaranteed to evoke ire. "How consistent of you, Nick. There was Sherrie from the airplane, now Brandi from the subway. Who will you meet next, I wonder? Margarita on the bus, perhaps?"

Nick arched his dark brows. "Anyone named Candy had better watch it," he said dryly, his gaze pinning her to the spot. And then he added in a low, whiskey-smooth voice, "Isn't that right, Sugar?"

Candy glowered at him. She felt scorched by sensual heat. Sugar. He called her that sometimes when he was teasing her. Sexually teasing her. In bed. It was their private joke, a *very* private joke. And now he dared to try to disconcert her by flaunting their bedroom secrets in front of her twin brother!

He'd succeeded, too; she was totally disconcerted. How could one word bring back a rush of memories so hot that she thought she was going to burn up? She remembered uninhibited things she and Nick had done together, the erotic intimacies, the outrageous whispers in the dark—

"Candy! You're not blushing?" Case was staring at her, transfixed.

He couldn't have looked more astonished if suddenly she were to have stripped naked. And that's how she felt. Stripped naked—exposed and vulnerable. And deeply wounded because Nick was here with her, only to be leaving her for a date with another woman. She began to tremble with the force of the emotions she fought to conceal.

"Of course I'm not blushing," she said tightly. "It's— it's rather stuffy in here, that's all." She laid an auntly hand on Shannon's chubby, pink cheek. "The baby is warm too. Let me get her a cold drink."

She pulled open the refrigerator door and removed a quart of milk, her movements tense and jerky. And then somehow, as she was opening the carton, it slipped from her hand. And somehow the contents ended up splattered all over Nick.

He let out a yelp as the cold liquid drenched him. "You threw that milk at me! On purpose!"

Candy stared at him, wide-eyed. He was wet and spluttering. "I—I didn't," she managed to say. She felt shaky and high-strung—and on the verge of breaking into a fit of uncontrollable giggles.

"You did it, Candy." Case marveled. "I saw the whole thing. You deliberately doused Nick with the milk." And then he began to chuckle. "Is there a grudge match going on here that I don't know about? If so, I'd have to say that Candy won this round."

"It was an accident. The carton slipped from my hand," Candy insisted. If she didn't get away, she was going to dissolve into laughter, adding insult to injury. "I—uh—I think I hear Tori. I'd better run upstairs and check on her." She dashed from the kitchen.

"Candace!" roared Nick. "Come back here!"

Tori was sound asleep in her crib, as Candy had known she would be. She hadn't really heard the baby, but she needed time and distance to regain her composure. The expression on Nick's face when the cold milk hit him had been priceless. And she really hadn't meant to spill it on him. Had she? Alone, in the darkness of the baby's room, Candy dropped her guard and permitted herself to grin.

She quickly recovered herself. If flinging that milk at Nick hadn't been a clumsy accident, then she was headed for big trouble. Never before had she lost her grip on herself long enough to actually act out her feelings. But tonight—tonight she'd been jealous and hurting and she couldn't hold it in. Nick had been standing there, sexy and virile and heartstoppingly masculine, evoking the most intimate of memories . . . *And he was dressed for a date with another woman!* Killing time talking with her brother until he left to pick up that Brandi creature!

Candy envisioned the other woman in her mind. Young, probably much younger than she. Blond and curvaceous, like Sherrie, that other bimbo with the alcohol name. The type who viewed public transportation as places to pick up men. A scheming airhead who read books on how-to-get-a-man and memorized the suggested ploys.

She heard voices in the entryway and then the front door slammed shut. Nick had gone. She closed her eyes as a shaft of pain rippled through her.

"Candy?" Case called softly from the hallway. Candy slipped quietly from the nursery. Case had come upstairs, a toast-munching Shannon perched happily on his hip.

"Tori is fine," she murmured unnecessarily. "She wasn't awake, after all."

"Nick left," said Case. He was studying her intently. "He had to change his clothes before he picked up—uh—what's her name, Daiquiri?"

Candy knew she was supposed to laugh. It was a brotherly joke. To her horror, tears swam in her eyes.

Case stared at her, as disconcerted as she was by the uncharacteristic tears. Case hadn't seen her cry since their kindergarten days. Not during their parents' ferocious fights all through their childhood, not during their mother's cruelty to her, and especially not over a man.

"Candy, you know how we Flynns are," he said uneasily, staring at the ground. "We don't talk about our emotions, about what we feel and why." He swallowed. "We never learned how to share things like that. The only person I've ever really been able to confide in is Sharla, but if—well, if you need to talk, I'll try and . . ." His voice trailed off. Though he appeared to be far more gregarious than she, his inward reserve was as strong as her own.

An emotionally charged silence descended. And then Shannon threw her mangled piece of zwieback to the floor. "All gone," she announced importantly.

"The comic relief," said Case with an indulgent smile for his daughter. "Look, Candy, I didn't mean to pry. I know that you—"

"I love him, Case," Candy blurted out. There, she'd said it aloud for someone else to hear. She'd finally admitted to another what she'd been fighting for years. She felt almost light-headed. With relief? Or was it fear? Perhaps a little of both.

"I've never stopped loving him," she added impulsively, unable to hide the truth any longer. "All these years . . . we've been together on and off. Mostly off, and that's my fault, Case. I've made such a mess of things. Now it's too late. There's too much water over the dam, and he—" A tiny sob escaped from her throat, but she forced herself to continue, to say the hurtful words aloud. "He doesn't want me anymore, Case. He doesn't love me."

Motionless, speechless, Case stared at her for a long moment. Candy watched him visibly search for something to say, and she felt a rush of sympathy for him. Poor Case. He was right, Flynns didn't share their feelings, and she'd just dumped decades worth of suppressed emotion on him. He was in shock. He undoubtedly wished he were anywhere but there.

"Sorry," she said, striving to achieve a note of lightness. And failing utterly. Her voice sounded as heavy as lead. "I guess I—"

"Why don't you think he wants you anymore?" Case interrupted slowly, staring thoughtfully at her. "How can you be sure that he doesn't love you?"

"He told me so." Candy stared at the carpet, feeling perilously close to breaking into sobs.

To her astonishment, Case laughed. "He told you so? Is that all?" He sounded inordinately relieved. He laughed again. "And you *believed* him?"

"It's true, Case. He—"

"You don't actually think that a man tells the woman he's in love with how he really feels, do you?" Case interrupted, scoffing. "I was crazy about Sharla from the day we met, but she had to drag it out of me."

"Well, I never had to drag it out of Nick. He's always been open and honest about his feelings."

"Hmm, bad move on his part," said Case. "But it seems he's wised up. He's not going to tell you how he really feels until he's sure of you. And from what I've seen here tonight, you haven't given him too many clues as to how you feel about him, Candy."

"How can I? Why should I? He has a date with Daiquiri from the subway, remember?"

Case's response was a wicked grin. "Yeah, I remember. He's taking her to Bennigan's; he mentioned it as he was leaving. C'mon, Candy, get Tori ready to go."

"Go where? She's sleeping, Case. I—"

"She can sleep in Bennigan's; babies that age can sleep anywhere. We're going out, Candy. You and me and Shannon and Tori are going to join Nick and his date. Crash their date, so to speak. *Ruin* their date."

Candy blushed. "No, Case, I can't." She couldn't think of anything more humiliating than to descend upon Nick and his date, with her brother and two babies in tow. Nick would know exactly what was going on; her pride simply couldn't handle—

"If you and Tori don't come along, then Shannon and I will do the dirty deed alone," Case said gleefully.

She'd seen that look on her brother's face before; it alarmingly mixed determination with deviltry. Case had always been a law unto himself when it came to social conventions.

"See you later," he said jauntily, starting down the stairs with Shannon.

"Bye-bye," called Shannon.

"No, wait!" Candy rushed into Tori's room, scooped up the sleeping infant in one arm, and snatched the packed diaper bag with the other. She heaved an exasperated groan as she followed her brother down the stairs. "I can't believe I'm going along with this preposterous scheme of yours. And that we're dragging two babies—who should be in their beds!—out to a night spot. I must be insane to let you talk me into this, Casey Flynn."

"You're in love," Case said, succinctly summing it up.

Five

Candy sat at the table in Bennigan's—the table that was far too small and crowded for their rather unorthodox party of six—and silently marveled that Case's fiendish plan was actually working. Nick's evening was being well and truly wrecked.

Part of her had not believed that her brother would actually go through with it. But Case proceeded to prove her wrong with a vengeance. After driving her and the two babies to Bennigan's, he'd propelled them right over to the very table where Nick sat with curvaceous Brandi, who was exactly as Candy had imagined her to be.

Greeting the couple effusively, Case pulled up some extra chairs, placed his hands on Candy's shoulders, and literally sat her in a seat before sprawling in one himself—much to Brandi's obvious consternation and to Nick's . . . what? What was his reaction to their appearance?

Candy, so adroit and perceptive in gauging behavior and reaction in the courtroom, had no idea what Nick thought of the Flynns' intrusion. There'd been a flicker in his dark eyes when she and Case had approached the table, but he'd greeted them smoothly, politely, giving no clues as to how he really felt. She hadn't dared even to glance at him when Case had plunked her into the chair. She'd concentrated solely on baby Tori, who hadn't stirred in her arms, despite the loud music, talk, and laughter.

She covertly studied Nick, who remained a total enigma as the evening wore on. He seemed willing enough to let Case completely dominate the conversation, which Case did in the most genially rude way, involving Nick and Candy in endless anecdotes about their high-school days—memories of antics, people, places, and music that obviously and totally excluded Brandi.

With all the subtlety of a runaway truck, Case next switched the topic of conversation to children, a subject guaranteed to bore a young, childless, single woman. And Brandi looked bored, her pretty face contorted with sulky petulance. Case talked at length about Shannon, then insisted on hearing all about little Nichole. The fact that both babies were the same age made it easy for the two proud fathers to exchange detailed information about their offspring. Candy ventured an occasional comment about Tori when asked, but unlike the men, she was unable to lose herself in the baby talk—not with the specter of Brandi seething in front of her eyes.

Tori continued to sleep peacefully, but Shannon made her presence felt. Though she was an exceedingly good-natured child, she was also an active toddler and intent on exploring her new surroundings. Or perhaps she was in league with her dad to sabotage Nick's date, for Candy had never seen her small niece so . . . busy. Shannon sat on the table, overturned drinks, and merrily threw the silverware to the floor. She climbed across the adults in their chairs and crawled around under the table, seemingly fascinated by the collection of feet and shoes to be found there. As luck would have it, she succeeded in pulling off one of Brandi's backless, high-heeled pumps, and then refused to give it up.

When Brandi testily suggested restraining the toddler, Case accused her of not liking children. "Why are you dating a man with a baby if you're so hostile toward little kids?" he demanded righteously.

Brandi spluttered a furiously incoherent reply. Nick said nothing, absolutely nothing.

Neither did Candy. She was appalled and embarrassed—*but* she silently admitted that she was delighted that Brandi had allowed herself to be turned into a peevish, pouting whiner whom Nick wouldn't want to date again. Here she was, Candace Flynn, a card-carrying feminist, engaged in a full-scale battle over a man and thrilled that the other woman was losing.

What was happening to her? she wondered nervously. A few years ago—last year!—she never would have permitted herself to become embroiled in such a debacle. Nor would she have told Case about Nick, or admitted to the despair and pain of losing him.

It was Shannon who provided a merciful end to the doomed date. Sitting in the middle of the table, tossing packets of sugar around, the little girl suddenly paused to yawn and rub her eyes.

"Shannon's sleepy," Case observed, and glanced at his watch. "It's nearly eleven o'clock, way past her bedtime. I'd better take her home and put her to bed."

"That's the best idea I've heard all night," Brandi muttered, scowling.

Case rose to his feet and picked up Shannon. "Torchy, old pal, you'll give Candy and Tori a lift home, won't you? I want to get Shannon to bed as soon as possible, and Candy's place is out of our way."

"Case!" Candy protested in horror. This was going too far! It was bad enough being here while Case blithely destroyed Nick's date, but to be left alone amid the wreckage was intolerable! She decided that she couldn't endure the humiliation. "I'll go with you!" she said, jumping up from her chair.

"Sorry, Sis." Case grinned at her, looking anything but sorry. Then he gently took the sleeping Tori from her arms and handed the baby to Nick.

Nick carefully accepted the small, warm bundle. Case called good-bye and strode away, with Shannon peering complacently over his shoulder. And Candy couldn't run after them, because her child was ensconced in Nick's arms.

Candace Flynn, redoubtable and fearless in the courtroom, fervently wished she would sink through the floor. She couldn't look at either Nick or Brandi. Nor could she think of a single reply when Nick stood up, Tori still cradled in his arms, and said calmly, but ever so dryly, "I think it's time we were all leaving."

There was complete silence in the car as they drove along the Capitol Beltway. Candy was in the backseat with Tori, who was strapped in her molded plastic safety seat, still sleeping soundly. She had no doubts that had Case been there, he would have managed to shove Brandi into the back while hustling Candy up front with Nick. Nevertheless, the date had been damaged beyond repair; Brandi's hostility toward Nick was almost palpable.

Nick seemed oblivious to his date's icy disdain. He made no apologies or attempts to smooth things over. When he dropped Brandi off at her apartment building, he didn't overrule her furious command not to bother seeing her to her door.

"Okay," he said with a shrug. " 'Bye, Brandi."

Brandi's reply was an unprintable expletive.

"Whew! Is she mad!" he observed as they watched her stalk into the building. "Well, who can blame her?" He switched on the radio, fiddling with the dial until he found the station he wanted.

Candy swallowed. It was time for the moment of reckoning, and she realized how very unprepared she was for it.

Nick turned around to face her. "Come sit up front, Candace," he said silkily. "I'm not going to let you cower back there any longer."

She rallied her defenses to bristle. "I'm not cowering. I happen to prefer sitting back here."

Nick gunned the engine. "You have till the count of three to get yourself up here, Candy. One—"

"Nick, please, I'd rather stay back here with the baby." Her voice quavered, and she suppressed a groan. Nick was right, she was cowering in the backseat like a wimp. And she sounded like one, too, using an infant as her defense. Better to brazen it out.

"Two," Nick said with an infuriatingly confident grin.

"I absolutely refuse to be bullied by you," she said haughtily, tilting her chin. "I'm staying here."

"Three." Nick opened his door.

Candy acted on pure reflex. She was out of the backseat and into the front before Nick had a chance to get out of the car.

"Good," he said approvingly, and caught her wrist. "Now come over here."

Aghast by her capitulation, Candy clung to the door handle. "I'll stay here, if you don't mind." She tried for a stern, no-nonsense approach, shooting him a look that had been known to make witnesses on the stand quiver.

Nick was not at all intimidated. "Oh, I do mind, Candace." He yanked her to the middle of the seat, close beside him. "Fasten your seat belt so we can get out of here."

She was in the center of the seat, snug against him. Their shoulders were touching, their thighs pressed together. Candy fastened the seat belt with trembling fingers. The heat emanating from his solid, masculine frame seemed to scorch her. The hot male scent of him filled her nostrils, affecting her like a potent drug. An aphrodisiac. A golden fire spread slowly through her. *Oh, Lord,* she thought dizzily. *Here we go again.*

The car moved smoothly through the darkened streets. Keeping her eyes straight ahead, Candy took a deep breath and murmured, "I want you to know that I'm completely mortified by what happened tonight, Nick. You have every reason to be furious with Case and me."

She knew she should apologize—she and her brother had willfully and wantonly ruined his evening. But she also knew that this was as close to an apology as she was going to come. For she wasn't at all sorry.

Nick gave a short laugh. "Yeah, my old buddy Case really outdid himself tonight. And, hey, little Miss Shannon was no slouch, either. How about when she dumped Brandi's piña colada into her shoe?"

"Shannon is just a baby, she didn't know what she was doing," Candy said, leaping to her niece's defense. "Your own child would've behaved exactly the same way, given the circumstances."

She thought of the nastily disapproving glares Brandi had directed at Shannon all evening and imagined her reacting the same way toward Nichole. At least Shannon had her father to protect her from the child-hating witches of the world, but who did poor little Nicki have? *Her* father dated them!

Candy scowled. "Anyway, why are you dating a woman who dislikes children, when you have a child yourself?"

"I never intended for Brandi to meet Nichole," Nick said mildly. "We're simply casual acquaintances. This was our first date."

Candy's lips curved into a smile. "And your last."

"It isn't polite to gloat, Candace."

"I wasn't gloating. I was . . . thinking."

"About what?"

Her smile broadened. "I had no idea that my brother could be such a crashing bore, rambling on forever about high school and Sharla and Shannon. Or that my darling little niece could be such a holy terror. It was quite an illuminating evening."

"I thought so too." His hand closed audaciously over her knee and slid slowly, purposefully, along the inside of her thigh.

The contact set off a shower of hot, sensual sparks in her abdomen. Candy struggled to maintain some semblance of composure. She was too keyed-up, as off balance as she'd ever been. She caught his wandering hand and firmly placed it back on the steering wheel.

Nick grinned. "You've been doing that for years."

"Since the first day you got your driver's license and took me for a ride in your cousin's car. You tried to put your hand under my skirt and almost crashed into a telephone pole."

"I remember that day." Nick chuckled. "I'll never forget your look of outrage when I touched your bare thigh. You told me to stop getting fresh—yes, *fresh*, that was the word you used—and to keep my mind on my driving and both my hands on the wheel."

"It's still good advice," Candy retorted primly, then spoiled the effect by smiling. He smiled back at her, and the years seemed to roll away, casting them both back in time, to another era they had shared.

She visualized the two of them as they'd been that early fall afternoon. Sixteen-year-old high-school juniors who cared deeply about each other and who were trying to cope with a potent physical attraction that simultaneously scared and excited them. She drifted easily into the past, swirling in a sea of memories. . . .

Those early years with Nick had been so turbulent, with joy and heartbreak inextricably woven together. She'd been in love and at war with the opposing drives within herself. She wanted Nick, but she was determined to avoid the trap of teenage pregnancy, which had ensnared her mother and so many of her classmates into a life of poverty and misery. She was intensely serious, relentlessly striving for academic perfection, dreaming of a life with money and position and respect. And Nick, raised in a conservative, traditional family, didn't understand her ambitions. They angered and confused him.

Her plans hadn't included love and marriage; Nick's did. They fought, they broke up and dated others, and then they made up, repeating the cycle over and over again through the years.

Nick was there for her college graduation. She remembered how proud he'd been of her. She still had the gold chain he'd given her for her Phi Beta Kappa key. She'd put it on and worn it all day and was still wearing it when they'd gone to her room in the dorm to spend the night together.

She was overcome by a landslide of sensual memories. In her mind's eye she saw herself lie down with him on the narrow bed, saw herself clinging to him, felt her body aching with arousal as they kissed. He caressed her intimately till she was twisting and moaning with need, and then came the sublime feeling of oneness as their bodies joined.

She had loved it, she had loved him. And for the first time she allowed herself to believe that perhaps things were going to work out for them, after all. She'd won a full scholarship to Georgetown University's School of Law in Washington, D.C., and Nick's opposition to her career seemed to have abated. He was even questioning whether or not he really wanted to spend his life in Detroit, working in the family store. He talked about looking for work in D.C., and maybe taking a few evening courses at one of the colleges there.

And then the outside world had cruelly intervened. Candy shivered, remembering the day that Nick had told her he was enlisting in the Marine Corps. If he didn't, he was sure to be drafted into the Army; either way, she knew he would wind up in Vietnam.

She had panicked. Though totally apolitical—she'd avoided the student demonstrators on campus, unable to understand their protestations against the establishment she was trying so hard to join—she was violently opposed to having Nick sent halfway across the globe *where he might be killed*!

She couldn't handle the thought of living in a world without Nick. The thought of losing him forever seemed to unleash something wild and reckless in her. She stopped being so cautious and started taking risks. And she ended up pregnant the month that Nick received orders to join the Marine unit in Da Nang. . . .

"What did you tell Case to make him decide to join Brandi and me at Bennigan's tonight?"

Nick's voice, amused and challenging, ripped into her reverie, catapulting her from the darkest year of her past into the present. After all the years, all the tears, here they were together, she thought, touched by the wonder of it. She wanted to tell him that she still loved him—after all, she'd taken the enormous step of telling her brother, hadn't she? Why couldn't she simply say those same words to Nick?

"C'mon, Counselor, I'm waiting for one of your masterfully evasive replies," Nick said softly, tauntingly. "Don't disappoint me."

She rallied herself to the task. "Maybe I told him that it was our duty to keep you from repeating your mistake with Sherrie with her nitwit counterpart. Is that masterfully evasive enough for you?"

"Not bad." His dark eyes gleamed. "It was certainly heroic of you and Case to come charging to my rescue."

She gave him an acid-sweet smile. "That's what friends are for."

"Now let's drop the fiction and get down to the facts, Candace." His voice deepened. "You finally told your brother about us, didn't you? And you also told him that you still want me."

Candy winced at his bluntness but didn't deny it. "Did you really prefer being with that Brandi creature rather than with me?" she countered softly. Hesitantly she laid a tentative hand on his thigh. Nick's hand immediately covered hers, and their fingers slowly, possessively, interlocked.

An evocative old ballad played on the radio. The singer's voice was ragged with pain and yearning as he pleaded, "Are you still mine?" Nick squeezed Candy's hand, and she closed her eyes and leaned her head against his shoulder.

She felt time and reason spinning away from her. "I need your love." The lyrics of the song heightened the emotional intensity that gripped her. Her nerves tingled, her pulse points throbbed. She felt as if she might fly apart from the sheer force of the sexual tension that pulsated between them.

Neither spoke a word until Nick braked the car to a stop. Candy felt as if she were emerging from a trance. She glanced slowly around her. "This isn't my house," she said somewhat dazedly.

"No, it's mine." Nick unlocked his seat belt but made no move to get out of the car. Instead, he turned toward her, stretching his arm along the back of the seat. He touched her face, tracing the smooth line of her jaw from her ear to her chin with his fingertips. "You're staying here with me tonight," he added huskily.

"I can't, Nick." She slid her arms slowly around his neck. "Tori—"

"You have enough stuff in that diaper bag to last Tori for a week." His hand slipped behind her neck and curved around it. He caressed the soft, creamy skin with long, lazy fingers. "You've got formula, bottles, baby food, diapers, clothes. What else could she possibly need?"

Lightly, affectionately, he brushed his nose against hers. She lifted her head and nibbled at his lips.

"She needs a place to sleep," Candy whispered against his mouth. "A *safe* place to sleep. She can roll over and has to have—"

"I have a portable crib set up for her in the den," Nick murmured. He kissed her lower lip, her upper lip, and the corners of her mouth in turn, his lips warm and soft and infinitely sensuous. "Complete with pink sheets and a white blanket with a pink-lamb pattern."

"You do?" Candy's fingers were stroking the hard, brown column of his neck. She drew back a little and gazed up at him, bemused.

He continued to caress her nape while he undid her seat belt with his other hand. He smoothed his palm over the flat softness of her stomach, then rested it on her waist. His fingers spanned the curve of her hip, and he kneaded lazily. "Ah, hell, Candy, I may as well admit it. I set up the crib before I came over to your place tonight. I knew the two of you would eventually end up here. If not tonight, then some other night soon. It was inevitable."

"Oh, was it?" She arched her dark brows, stiffening. "Even though you haven't called me? Even though you made a date with a—a tramp you picked up on the Metro?"

He gave a low, sexy laugh. "I couldn't let you get too sure of yourself, now could I, Judge Flynn?"

A sudden bolt of anger flashed through her. "Do you mean you weren't serious when you told me that it was finally all over between us?" *She had been suffering while he*— "You were merely playing games?"

"Uh-oh." He grinned at her, thoroughly unrepentant. "I can see the fire in those big green eyes. Sweet Candy is ticked off."

She tried to pull away from him. "You're damn right I am! And I have every reason to be. Let me go, Nick, I'm—"

With a coolly possessive air, he pulled her into him and positioned her against his hard, masculine frame. "You're not going anywhere, baby. You're already committed." He slid one big hand upward and settled it just below the underside of her breast. "There's no turning back now."

And then his mouth came down fiercely on hers.

The sensual impact of his lips on hers unleashed all of her pent-up emotions in full force. Her mouth opened under his, and she felt the hot thrust of his tongue, velvety and insistent, probe the moist, inner softness. She had wanted him, needed him, loved him for so long—and she'd been so afraid that she never would have him again. A small, soft moan escaped from her throat, and Candy's body surged into his.

His hand shifted to gently cup her breast, and the erotic, circular motion of his thumb on her nipple sent shock waves of sensation through her. The silky material of her blouse and her thin, lacy teddy offered no protection from the exquisitely sensual pressure.

Candy whimpered with pleasure and clung closer. Their kiss deepened, becoming more intimate, more demanding. Her mind clouded and yielded completely to her senses, which were full of the taste and feel and scent of him. When his lips left hers to trail a path of biting little kisses along the curve of her neck, she tilted her head to give him easier access.

"Candy." He groaned her name, burying his lips in the soft, scented hollow of her neck. Her breast was warm and soft in his hand, the tight nipple pressing against his palm. An ever-rising urgency fueled his sensual hunger. "Darling, I've been waiting for you, wanting you for so damn long." His voice echoed the yearning she felt, the pain and the frustration too.

"Then why—" She moved her hands restlessly over him. "Why haven't you called me, Nick? It's been two whole weeks . . ." Her voice trailed off, and she slipped her fingers between the buttons of his shirt, seeking the warm delights of his skin.

"The phone works both ways, Candy." He gazed down at her passion-flushed face with serious dark eyes.

"You were waiting for me to call you first?"

He shrugged. "There have been times when we've gone two *years* or more without seeing each other," he reminded her. "How was I to know that you considered two *weeks* apart—"

"Unbearable," Candy finished for him.

"Unbearable," he echoed. He caressed her earlobe with the pad of his thumb, stroking over the small gold stud and fondling the soft flesh with a sensual expertise that sent shivers of sensation streaking through her body.

She caught her breath. "Why do we play these torturous games with each other, Nick?"

He heaved a sigh. "Honey, I wasn't playing a game. I didn't know that you were hoping I'd call. As usual, we hadn't parted on the best of terms and I was waiting—"

"For what?"

"Until I couldn't handle it anymore. Until I couldn't stand being away from you a second longer. Until I was half out of my mind with wanting you. Believe me, baby, I was getting close to that state. I tried to lose myself in work, I tried concentrating on my child, tried looking for . . . er, other female companionship. But it wasn't working, Candy. As much as I rebelled against it, I knew I was going to have to see you again sooner or later."

"Although I suppose you hoped it would be later rather than sooner?" she asked dryly.

"You know how it is with us," he said, shaking his head with an air of resignation. "We have a boomerang relationship. We cast off in different directions but end up right back where we started every time. Together."

She followed the well-shaped lines of his mouth with her fingertips. "And is that so bad?" she asked huskily.

"It's hell." He trapped her hand, tracing each finger with his lips, with his tongue, then pressed her palm against his open mouth. "Sweet, sweet hell."

"Nick." She gasped as a sharp coil of desire wound tighter and tighter inside her. "Oh, Nick, I want you so much."

"I know." He smiled down at her, and her heart leapt at the warmth she saw reflected in his dark, dark eyes. "But I didn't think that you'd come after me, with your brother and his child in tow, to stake your claim on me. That was a most un-Candy-like move, my sweet."

"You're mine," she said, surprising herself as much as him with her words and the possessive fierceness of her tone. She captured his head in her hands and brought it down to hers, brushing her mouth lightly, temptingly, over his. The tip of her tongue slipped out to tease his lips apart, then slid into the warmth of his mouth to rub seductively against the velvety roughness of his tongue.

With a muffled groan he took control of the kiss, of

the embrace, and Candy surrendered gladly, reveling in his strength and mastery.

They kissed wildly, rapaciously, the unslaked passion burning and building between them. Candy felt the hard muscles of Nick's body against her, his masculinity complementing her feminine softness. She'd endured many nicknames during her legal career— barracuda, man-eater, and castrating bitch being some of the more complimentary ones—but Nick had always made her feel alluring and feminine and soft. With him, and him alone, she was a giving, passionate woman who surrendered lovingly, unconditionally, to her man.

"Let's go inside." Nick paused to kiss her deeply one last time. He pulled away from her to swing open the car door.

"You don't feel like recapturing our wild and crazy youth by making love in the car?" Candy laughed up at him.

"I won't even dignify that with a response." He reached down to take her hands and hauled her out of the car. His hands slid over her lush, feminine curves and came to rest on her hips, twisting her against him. "Let's go to bed, Candace."

Six

After placing baby Victoria in the portable crib and tucking the white blanket with the pink-lamb pattern on it around her, Nick took Candy's hand and led her along the darkened hall of the rambling, one-story house.

"Lillian, Nichole's nanny, has that room," Nick whispered, pointing to a closed door on the left. "And that's Nicki's room on the right."

His daughter's door was open, and a small night-light cast shadows on the wall. Candy automatically started in to check on the child. Nick followed her. They stood beside the white crib, looking down at the baby, Nick standing close behind Candy.

Nichole was sprawled across her crib with an awesome assortment of stuffed animals competing for space around her. "Why is she sleeping in her clothes?" Candy whispered, her gaze sweeping the baby's yellow overalls and printed jersey.

"She was out like a light before there was time to change her into pajamas." Nick smiled down at the sleeping child. "Nicki isn't a night owl like Shannon."

Nicki stirred slightly and slipped her thumb into her mouth. Candy leaned down to stroke the soft, blond, baby curls. From the time she'd been a child of ten, the helplessness and innocence that babies possessed always evoked a strong response in her, and Candy felt that familiar, protective warmth suffuse her as she gazed at Nick's daughter. "She's a beautiful child, Nick," she said softly.

"Yes." Nick wrapped his arms around her waist and pulled her back against him. He leaned down to brush his lips against the dark silk of her hair.

"Oh, Nick," she murmured, laying her hands over his. Her skin was hot and tingling, her nerves jumpy with anticipation. There was a yearning ache deep within her, which grew and throbbed as he kissed her neck, as he fondled her breasts. She was hungry for him, needing him in a primitive, elemental way that threatened to snap the last of her tenuous control.

She turned in his hold and gazed up at him. Even in the shadowy night she could see the desire in his eyes. His pupils were huge and dilated, seeming to merge with the midnight darkness of his eyes. She saw the pulse throbbing in his throat and reached up to kiss him there.

Slipping his arm around her shoulder, Nick settled her snugly against his side and walked out of the room with her. He paused to kiss her lingeringly at the threshold of his bedroom.

Candy responded with all the passion and depth of her love for him, tightening her arms around him and pressing her body intimately against his powerful, masculine heat.

When he lifted his mouth from hers, he held her tightly and kissed his way to her throat. "When I'm with you, I lose my head," he murmured between kisses. "So while I'm still in control of my thought processes, I'd better ask if you're still using your diaphragm or if you want me to take precautions."

Candy's eyes widened. Obviously she'd already lost control of her own mental processes. For the second time in her life she hadn't given a thought to the consequences of unprotected lovemaking. She gulped.

That first time, Nick hadn't, either. And she'd become pregnant with their child, who hadn't lived to be born.

"I—I don't have it," she said, stammering. "I never expected tonight to end this way."

He raised his brows. "Didn't you?"

"Of course not! You hadn't called me, remember? And when you dropped by, you were quick to tell me about your date."

"Uh-oh, here it comes. Another lecture on my shortcomings as a suitor. Candy, sweetheart, this is neither the time nor the place. You've answered my question. I'll take care of us."

Another time, another place, Candy might have escalated the incident into a full-scale conflict. In the past she hadn't been able to walk away from a possible quarrel; victory and supremacy were all-important to her then. But no longer. She wanted to give, not to win.

"Nick," she said softly, stroking his cheek with her slender fingers, "I didn't expect tonight to end this way, but I'm so glad that it did."

"So am I, love." He hugged her. "So am I."

He pulled her blouse loose from the waistband of her slacks, and she watched him deftly undo the red, silk-covered buttons and slip it from her shoulders. Her slacks were the next to go, and he divested her of them with the same smooth expertise. She felt oddly, dreamily passive as he undressed her. A syrupy warmth coursed through her as she stood before him under his dark, possessive gaze.

Nick took a step back to study her in her bright, red silk teddy. The musky, feminine scent of her perfume lingered in his nostrils. A spasm of desire rippled through him. Passionate memories of all their other times together washed over him like fire. There had never been a woman in his life, his heart, his bed, to equal Candy.

"You're so beautiful," he murmured rawly, "and so damn sexy, I feel as if I'm going to explode."

Her breasts, full and round, perfectly filled the cups of her teddy. He traced its outline with his fingertips, then centered on the lacy cups, teasing her nipples through the delicate material. Candy shuddered with need. His warm, hard palms cupped her bottom, kneading the rounded firmness with a rhythm that made her moan and move sinuously into his hands.

"Oh, Nick, it's been so long," she whispered on a breathless sigh. "I thought we'd never be together again, and I missed you so. There have been times when I wanted you so much, I thought I would die of it."

"I know, love, it's been the same for me," he said in a raspy tone.

They kissed hungrily, his tongue filling her mouth as he wanted to fill her body, stroking slowly and deeply. His hands moved over her in urgent sweeps, matching the rhythmic pressure of his mouth. She responded with a twisting, sensual movement of her hips that inflamed him.

Unable to wait a moment longer to touch him, she helped him pull off his clothes, her hands trembling as she touched the hard, smooth warmth of his skin. She combed her fingers through the thick mat of wiry hair that darkened his chest, then followed the downward path of it lower, lower, where she found him pulsing with his need for her.

"That's like pouring gasoline on an open fire." He groaned softly, catching her hands and repositioning them around his neck. "We have to slow down, sweetheart. I want to make it last, I want it to be good for you."

She smiled at him, her cheeks hot and red with emotion. "It's always good with you, Nick. *You're* good for me."

"Ah, Candy." His voice was thick with passion. He gathered her to him for another deep, devastating kiss. Still kissing, he lowered her to the bed and slipped his thigh between her legs. Yearning and pliant, Candy arched her body into his. She rubbed her breasts, swollen and full beneath the red lace against his hair-rough chest. Nick picked up on her sensual cue and deftly lowered the straps of the teddy.

Her breasts were aching for his hands, and he massaged them gently, sensuously, before closing his mouth over one dusky rose nipple. He laved the tight bud with his lips and tongue until Candy cried out his name and buried her fingers in the thick darkness of his hair, holding his head to her. Her breathing was shallow and rapid, and she wrapped her legs tightly around the solid column of his thigh, seeking sensual relief for the burgeoning needs he'd aroused in her.

He caressed the white softness of her belly with one big hand, dipping into the hollow of her navel to trace it with his thumb. She inhaled sharply and held her breath as his fingers moved lower to brush the dark, tight curls.

"Nick, please," she whispered helplessly, opening her thighs to him.

Their eyes locked. Holding her gaze, he stripped her teddy from her with one downward sweep. His fingers rubbed between her legs with exquisite sensuality, finding the melting warmth, the incredible softness of her.

"So hot and sweet," he murmured, caressing her intimately, skillfully, unlocking all the flowering secrets of her femininity. "So wet and welcoming for me."

He was driving her out of her head with the delicious pleasure he so masterfully gave to her. Candy clung to him, running her hands over him, relearning the virile textures of his body. An explosive combination of memory and anticipation filled her, shattering in its intensity.

"Now, Nick," she cried. "Love me now."

With a low, sexy sound, he prepared to do just that, then thrust slowly into her. She felt him fill her, hot and hard and hungry, and she clutched at him, digging her burgundy-polished nails into his back. It had been a long time and it hurt a little, but she drew in a sharp breath and didn't make a sound.

But Nick, always so aware and attuned to her, immediately picked up on her reaction. "Am I hurting you, baby?" he murmured, his onyx eyes wide with concern.

"A little," she whispered. "It's been so long, Nick. . . ." Her voice rose slightly as her body began to melt, to accommodate itself to his virile strength. She closed her eyes and shivered as he began to move in a slow, easy rhythm. Hot ripples of pleasure radiated through her body, and she clung to him, throbbing, aching.

"There's been no one else?" he asked, staring down at her with pure masculine possession. "Since when?"

She could have told him that he had no right to ask and refused to answer. It was the way she'd handled similar questions in the past. To tell him the truth would give away so much, would reveal all of what she felt for him. But once again she gave no thought to winning. Only to giving.

"Not since the last time we were together," she admitted quietly. "When I told you about my appointment to the bench."

"And we had one of the most monumental fights in our history," Nick added, his voice tinged with regret.

A sharp little flash of pain ripped through her. Emotional, not physical. For she remembered that the next time she'd seen Nick after that monumental fight had been at their high-school reunion. She'd gone with the express purpose of making up with him, of trying to work things out at last. She'd worn her diaphragm in preparation . . . and he'd arrived with Sherrie. Her pride had been decimated, and she'd covered by acting the virago.

A dark flush tinged her cheeks and she swallowed hard. Nick bent to kiss her tenderly. "It's in the past, darling. Let's put it behind us."

Her green eyes searched his. "Yes," she whispered. "Oh, Nick, yes!" Clinging to him, she moved sensually beneath him and watched his face dissolve into ecstasy.

Their bodies moved together in a timeless, magical rhythm, her liquid heat enveloping him as the rapture grew stronger, as all reason was replaced by stunning physical sensation. Desire and passion and need joined into a surging force that swept them into a vortex of mindless, yearning tension that exploded suddenly, sending them both into a realm of wondrous pleasure.

Nick collapsed against her, burying his head in the hollow of her shoulder, and Candy hugged him tightly to her. Their bodies still joined, they shared kisses and love words as they slowly drifted back to earth.

Languid and mellow in the sweet aftermath of their passion, it was easy for her to say the words usually held in check by her wary reserve. She felt so close to him. Only with Nick did she ever approach the blissful state of true intimacy. "I love you, Nick." She kissed his neck, stroking his hair, his face, with loving hands. "Never let me go again."

"Maybe we should put that in writing," he said lightly, his eyes gleaming with humor. "Do you think such a document would hold up in court, Your Honor?"

Candy managed a smile. His lighthearted mood didn't match her own. She felt intense, earnest, seriously committed. She wanted him to return her declaration of love. She wanted his dark gaze to be deep and soulful, not brimming with amusement. She wanted him to—her heart seemed to stop and then start again at double time—she wanted him to ask her to marry him. Again. And this time, for the first time ever, she knew that her answer would be an unqualified yes.

But Nick didn't say those magic words. He kissed her temple, then carefully withdrew from her, rose, and went into the bathroom. When he returned and lay down on his back, Candy snuggled close, resting her head on his shoulder, slipping one leg over his. His arms came around to tuck her against him, and he closed his eyes with a sigh of contentment.

Candy's brows narrowed. Was he going to fall asleep?

"Nick," she prodded. "It was wonderful tonight, wasn't it?"

Nick smiled, his eyes still closed. "You know it was, sweetheart." He stroked her idly, almost absently. "The best."

Candy frowned slightly. He was hardly waxing poetic about the experience. It had been so long, and she had given herself to him completely, without reservation. Didn't he even care to comment on that?

Apparently not. "Good night, honey," he mumbled sleepily.

"You're going to sleep?" she asked incredulously.

"I'm exhausted, Candy. I've been up since six this morning. You must be tired too. Close your eyes and go to sleep."

This was not going the way she'd planned. Here she was, ready to commit herself to Nick at last, ready to fulfill his lifelong dream . . . and he wanted to sleep?

And then, unbidden, came a terrible thought. What if marrying her was no longer his lifelong dream? The cruel irony of the situation was not lost on her. Nick had wanted to marry her for years, and for years she'd assiduously refused. She'd run the gamut of excuses, citing her studies, her career, her lack of faith in lasting marriages. Left unspoken had been her terror of being trapped and dependent in a relationship that brought only pain, but Nick had known about that, too, and had tried to reassure her. All to no avail. And now, now when she was finally strong enough and brave enough to risk all her doubts and fears for love and accept the challenge of marriage, Nick wasn't asking.

A sudden flashback chilled her. Two weeks ago, when she'd met Nick in Babyland, he had announced flatly that he would never propose to her again, that he'd decided that marriage wasn't for him. She had thought at the time that he was needling her. But suppose he weren't? Suppose all he wanted from her was what they'd just shared? Sex.

A spasm of dread coursed through her, prompting her to immediate action. "Nick." She propped herself up on one elbow and stared down at him. He opened his eyes and their gazes locked. Impulsively she cast aside all pride and dared to reveal her insecurity and self-doubt. "Nick, don't you . . ." she paused and swallowed. "Don't you love me anymore?"

He reached up to stroke the flushed softness of her cheek. "Honey, do you even have to ask? You know I do. You've always known," he added with a wry smile.

Once again the lightness of his tone disturbed her. He seemed almost . . . detached. She tried to rally her logic and common sense to strike down the anxieties that loomed ominously in her mind.

But logic and common sense proved to be cold comfort when her heart was bursting with the need to share her burgeoning feelings of love.

"I wanted to hear you say it, Nick," she confessed with a sheepish little smile. "Sometimes it's nice to hear the words."

"That comes as something of a surprise, Candace." His voice, his smile, made her shiver. "I was under the impression that you found the words an annoyance. A demand put upon you that you didn't want or ask for."

She stared at him in dismay. His voice was light and wry, his attitude dry and distant. Why was he erecting this barrier between them? Why was he holding back?

And then a crushing realization began to dawn. In the past Nick had felt the way she had felt tonight. Open and vulnerable. Intense, earnest, and seriously committed. Her muscles clenched, her whole body going rigid.

She'd known it, had come to take it for granted, but she'd never really understood how it felt until tonight, when she'd given him everything and wanted the depth and intensity of her commitment returned.

But the tables had been turned. Now he was the one to withhold and draw back to preserve a safe emotional distance between them.

She couldn't blame him, Candy admitted to herself. In the past she *had* come to dread hearing "I love you" from him because she knew that a marriage proposal usually followed his impassioned declaration. And she hadn't wanted marriage. Not until now. She'd always pushed him away.

Casting a quick glance at Nick, she saw that he had closed his eyes again. His breathing was deep and even, and he appeared to be asleep. Sleep, the ultimate withdrawal.

But Candace Flynn was not one to meekly accept what fate threw her way. She reached down to pull the sheet and lightweight blanket over them, then cuddled close to Nick.

"I love you, Nick Torchia," she whispered, and he stirred softly and tightened his arms around her. She wondered if he was awake and merely feigning sleep. If so, he may as well hear her out. "And we *are* going to get married."

He didn't react. Perhaps he really was asleep. Saying the words aloud clarified and strengthened her resolve. She was going to marry Nick and raise his child as her own, just as he would raise her little Tori as his own daughter.

His own daughter . . . A chill of foreboding sliced through her. What was Nick going to say when she revealed the bit of deceptive handiwork hidden away in the box under her bed? She thought about waking him and telling him now, then decided against it. Their newfound peace was still too fragile to risk. She would tell him later and he would understand. She would make him understand.

In the past her character, her talents, and her other qualities had all been subordinated to her career ambitions. Now she would channel all of that, all of herself, into her personal life. Into her relationship with Nick.

Her goal was to be his wife, and she possessed a powerful resolve that had never been defeated. When

Candace Flynn set her wits on getting something, nothing or no one had ever been able to stop her.

Time seemed to crawl by. Candy tossed and turned fitfully as she stared into the darkness, her mind racing. She'd always had difficulty sleeping; her energy level was too high, her mind too active to easily cede control of consciousness and relax into sleep. And sleeping in a bed and a bedroom that wasn't her own exacerbated the problem. She was a creature of rigid habits and routines; she missed her goose-down pillow, her small plastic fan that circulated the air, and her special black window shades that blocked out all outside light.

Eventually her restless fidgeting awakened Nick. "This is like trying to sleep on a trampoline," he complained with a sleepy groan. "Settle down and go to sleep, Candy."

She sat up in bed. "I can't, Nick. Maybe I'd better go home. I'll never get to sleep here, and I'm keeping you awake."

Yawning, Nick struggled to sit up. He reached for her. "Still plagued by insomnia, hmm?" He cradled her against his chest, and she nodded and relaxed against him, laying her head on his shoulder. "You're supposed to sink blissfully into a deep sleep after a session of mind-blowing sex, Candace," he pointed out.

"I've heard that myth."

"But it doesn't seem to work that way for you," Nick said knowingly. "You tend to get even more charged up. And when you're not in your own bed with the extra-firm mattress and your special pillow and blanket and fan—not to mention those deadly shades on your windows that gives your room all the ambience of a crypt—sleeping becomes a virtual impossibility."

She laughed. "You know all my idiosyncracies, Nick."

"Too well," he agreed, heaving an exaggerated sigh.

"I guess Sherrie didn't have any—uh—eccentricities when it came to sleeping. She probably could hop into any bed anywhere and be asleep the moment her dim little head hit the pillow."

"That's about it."

There was a long moment of silence. They lay together, the darkness surrounding them like a protective screen. And then: "I hated it when you married her, Nick. I felt as if my heart had been ripped out." It was easier to reveal herself in the concealing cloak of darkness.

"But you never let on," Nick said quietly. "I didn't think it mattered to you."

"It mattered, Nick. It hurt more than words can ever describe."

"I didn't get married just to hurt you, Candy. I really did think it was over between us, and I wanted my life to go forward. I'd spent too much time bogged down in our past."

"I don't blame you for thinking that." She swallowed hard. "I'd said some terrible things to you during that last fight we had—you know, when you advised me to stick with my practice and turn down the judgeship. Nick, I'm so sorry for everything I said that night."

"I'm the one who should apologize for inflicting my opinions on you in that matter, Candy. I was obviously wrong. You're doing well as a judge, so well that you have a crack at hearing one of the most important cases ever to be heard in the county."

"No, Nick, you were absolutely right," she blurted out. "I'm not doing well as a judge. I'm an *average* judge. And I'm bored to death with it, for all the reasons you cited. Giving up my practice was the second worst mistake of my life. The first was letting you marry another woman."

Nick's arms tightened around her. He was astounded by her admission. Candy was not one for acknowledging mistakes, expressing regret, or apologizing—nor admitting to feelings of hurt and jealousy. Yet she'd just done all of those things. Her openness and vulnerability touched him deeply, for Candace Flynn had exe-

cuted a lifetime policy of not being open or vulnerable
. . . until now.

His thoughts drifted to their lovemaking earlier.
It had been as passionate as ever, but there had
been something more. Her impenetrable core of reserve, which enabled her to keep a part of herself
aloof even from him in their most intense moments,
finally had been dissolved. It was the first time she'd
said "I love you" without qualifying those words, without adding conditions. He knew that if he had asked
her to marry him—as he had so many other times—her
answer would have been yes.

So why hadn't he asked her? Nick's lips twisted in a
grim smile of irony. Because he'd meant what he had
said to her that afternoon in Babyland. He had no
intentions of marrying again. Once burned, twice shy,
as the old cliché went—and he'd been burned, all right.

He recalled the tense, hostile days of his ill-fated
marriage, how he'd hated to go home, how he and
Sherrie could scarcely tolerate being in the same room
with each other. Thankfully Nichole hadn't been born
yet and had been spared living even a day in that
poisonous atmosphere.

And he intended to keep it that way. He'd seen the
detrimental effect living in such an environment had
had on Candy and vowed that his own child would
never have to suffer a similar fate.

Ironically, after fighting over it all these years, he'd
finally come around to Candy's point of view, he mused.
It was better to live alone in peace than in a marriage
of hate—and too many marriages degenerated to that
sorry state. How strange that Candy seemed to have
changed her mind about marriage, just as he'd changed
his.

"You're so quiet," Candy whispered. "What are you
thinking, Nick?"

When he didn't reply at once, she knew he was working on a tactful answer to give to her, one that wouldn't
hurt or anger her as his true thoughts would.

Nick shifted her in his arms, tilting her chin upward to brush her mouth with his. "I was thinking that I'm glad you're here with me, even if you *are* keeping me awake. You're definitely worth staying awake for."

And that was true, he added to himself. He'd never wanted any woman the way he wanted Candy, and she wanted him just as intensely. There was no reason why they couldn't enjoy this interlude, and whatever followed it, as two mature adults. There was no reason why great sex had to be parlayed into anything more than exactly what it was.

"Smooth, Nick." Sadness streaked through her. He wasn't smooth in the past. He used to be demanding and impassioned and sincere. "Those words could be said by anyone to anyone. I want to know what you're *really* thinking—about us."

"Don't push, honey," he said lightly.

"That's what I always used to say to you." Her voice trembled. "I just want to know where we stand." She caught her lip between her teeth and held it there. "And—and that's what you always used to say to me, isn't it?" She felt like crying.

He didn't answer. He wasn't going to say the words she wanted to hear, and they both knew it. She remembered all those times she had said to him, "I love you, but . . ." Now he was saying it to her.

"Candy, sweetheart, relax," he said soothingly as he gently stroked her hair. "We're here together, and that's all that matters for now. Let's just enjoy the time we have with each other. You know how much I want you, how much I care about you."

Candy was struck again by a chilling sense of déjà vu. They had played this scene before, with her speaking the lines that he now spoke. She turned her face into his chest and clung to him. She felt drained and passive, unable to do anything but lay quietly and accept his comforting caresses.

Which soon escalated into something else. He ran his hands over her body, enjoying the feel of her supple curves, the smooth warmth of her creamy skin. His kisses and caresses soon roused her to vibrant passion, and he gloried in the explosive lack of control that made her arch and cling to him as he took her. He began to stroke within her, building the exquisite rhythm to an almost unbearably rapturous heat, and Candy moved with him.

A soft, wild cry tore from her throat, and she reveled in his possession of her. She was irrevocably his, and he belonged just as irrevocably to her, she thought dizzily, as she drifted back to earth, feeling cherished and safe in his arms. They had hurt each other in the past, but she would make him realize that their future together would be one of mutual love and happiness. She had to make him realize it!

The first lights of dawn had streaked the sky when an indignant wail sounded from the vicinity of the den. Candy lay on her stomach, her face buried in the pillow, and she resisted the urge to put it over her head. She'd finally fallen into a deep, dreamless sleep about two hours ago. She groaned when the baby's cry summoned her again.

Nick sat up, obviously still half asleep. "I'm coming, Nicki," he mumbled on a yawn.

"Nick, it's Tori who's awake. You can go back to sleep," said Candy, swinging her legs over the side of the bed. She scanned the room for her clothes. They were scattered on the floor. "May I borrow a robe?"

He handed her a robe, then donned one himself and followed her into the den where Tori was lying on her back in the crib, kicking her arms and legs and verbalizing her displeasure through an assortment of noises, ranging from an impatient cry to a rather commanding shriek. When she spotted Candy, her small face lit with a smile and she issued a pleased squeal.

Nick reached into the crib and picked her up. "Hello, little lady," he said softly. "Were you surprised to wake up in a strange bed?"

Tori grinned and gurgled at him. Her winsome innocence charmed him, and he smiled at the child. And then it struck him for the first time. The baby's eyes were a different color, but that smile . . . it was pure Candy. And the casual feelings of fondness he had for a cute baby abruptly escalated into something more. He felt connected to this child. Protective. Paternal?

Candy took the baby from him and deftly cleaned and changed her, talking to her all the while. The baby babbled cheerfully in response. Nick watched them silently, intently.

"I'll give Tori her bottle while you take a shower and dress," he volunteered. "Nichole won't be awake for a little while yet."

"Will her nanny be shocked to find me here?" Candy asked bluntly. "Or are there often women around your place in the morning?"

"Careful, Candace. I'm liable to think you're jealous if you don't resort to a more subtle line of questioning."

"I *am* jealous." Her eyes met his. "Of any woman who ever meant anything to you. I've always felt possessive of you, Nick, but I—I've always tried to play it cool." Her voice lowered. "It was my utmost priority, Lord knows why."

"You're not playing it cool now, Candy."

"Because I can't. I don't want to, Nick. After last night . . . well, you know how I feel about you, and I *want* you to know. I love you, Nick. I want us to be together." Her eyes pleaded with him.

Nick stared at her. How was he supposed to resist? He couldn't, he didn't want to. He heaved a sigh. "You're the only woman I've brought home since Nichole's birth, Candy. I'd never submit my child to a revolving-door procession of women at the breakfast table."

Candy smiled, her face radiant. Nick may have temporarily changed his mind about marrying her, but she still retained a special place in his heart. He didn't mind having *her* at the breakfast table with his child.

She handed the baby to him. "She likes her formula

lukewarm," she instructed. "And she likes this bottle with the blue nipple, and—"

"We'll manage just fine. I know a thing or two about giving bottles to babies, you know."

"I know you do." She stood on tiptoe to kiss his cheek. Her breast pressed against the muscular strength of his arm, and an electrical current seemed to pass through them both.

Their eyes met. "Later, Candace," he promised firmly. She nodded, her heart suddenly lighter than air.

Seven

Later that afternoon Candy called Nick from her judge's chambers where she was studying the briefs filed by opposing counsel in an incompetency hearing, perhaps her least favorite area of family law, and one she'd been able to avoid assiduously in her own divorce practice. The turgid prose was stupefying, a guaranteed headache-inducer. Candy massaged her aching temples with her fingers. The most incompetent thing about these briefs was the lawyers who'd written them. She could just imagine the tedium of the trial.

She decided that she deserved a break and dialed the TSI office.

"Candy!" Nick sounded astonished to hear her voice. "Is there something wrong?" he added, immediately concerned.

She could hardly blame him for thinking that she wouldn't call unless it was a dire emergency. In the past she'd never called him simply to chat. Or to ask him out. Candy clenched the phone tightly. It wasn't easy breaking a lifetime pattern of playing it cool, but she was determined to start.

"The only thing wrong is that I miss you," she said softly.

Nick smiled and relaxed. "Do you?"

"You're supposed to say that you miss me, too, Torch."

"I do. You made a great hit with Lillian this morning, you know. No one can be more charming than you when you choose to be, Candy. She was singing your praises till I walked out the door. She was quite taken with Tori too."

"I'm glad. I liked her very much. She's wonderful with Nicki." Candy took a deep breath. "Nick, I was wondering if you and Nicki would like to come over to my place for dinner tonight."

He hesitated before answering. "You want Nicki and me to come for dinner? Are you sure you aren't suggesting something else, Candy?"

Was he flirting with her? Testing her? She tried to weigh the evidence but found the analysis time-consuming and tedious. It was far better to react sharply and directly with a question of her own. Once again the lawyer within her won out against the judge. "What are you trying to say to me, Nick?"

"That I'll bring Nichole to your place for dinner, if that's what you want, but we won't stay the night. I don't want my child spending her nights anywhere but in her own crib in her own room in her own house. If your invitation to dinner is really a veiled invitation for me to sleep with you, then I'll come over later, after I've put the baby to bed."

She glanced down at the typewritten pages before her. The print blurred before her eyes and she blinked. Her temper flared like a grenade at the moment the pin was pulled. "If you're trying to enrage me, you've succeeded beyond your wildest expectations." Instead of rising in anger, her voice had lowered ominously.

"Candy, I simply want to set some guidelines. There aren't just the two of us to consider anymore, you know. There are four people involved, two of them children. We each have a baby and— "

"Thank you for pointing that out to me. You have a remarkable grasp of the obvious. I also find it interesting that your concern for our children didn't preclude you from whisking Tori and me to your place last night, nor did you have any scruples about *my* baby spending the night in a crib in a room in a house that wasn't hers."

"Candy, you're overreacting. I—"

"You can consider my dinner invitation rescinded. While Nichole is always welcome in my home, you, Nicholas Anthony Torchia, most definitely are not." She replaced the receiver forcefully in its cradle.

She was too angry to resume her study of the tedious incompetency briefs. She couldn't sit still; her energy and anger needed a physical outlet. She began to pace back and forth in front of her desk. How dare he? She paced faster. No one could infuriate her more than Nick. Or hurt her more. She scowled. How had that unguarded thought escaped from the suppression chamber of her mind?

There was a quick, tentative knock at the door. Candy stopped pacing. As no one was admitted to judges' chambers unscreened, she knew it had to be either her secretary or her law clerk. She hoped for Sally, her secretary. "Yes?"

"Judge Flynn?" The door opened and Jack Conrad, her law clerk, poked his head in. "I hate to disturb you . . ." Jack's standard opening. She made him nervous, she knew. He always approached her tentatively, with an escape route seemingly in the back of his head should he need it.

His wary caution toward her was undeserved, Candy thought indignantly. She'd never given him any reason to be afraid of her; she'd always behaved with judgely decorum in her staff's presence. Sally wasn't afraid of her. Her eyes narrowed to slits. "You're not disturbing me, Jack. What is it?"

"J-Judge Wright is here to see you, sir. I mean, ma'am! Judge Flynn."

Judge Roger Wright entered to see Jack's hasty exit. He stared quizzically at Candy.

"I'm Farmer MacGregor to his Peter Rabbit," she explained, borrowing a reference from her nephews' favorite storybook. "Am I really *that* scary, Roger?"

He laughed. "Only when you're the opposing counsel. And those days are gone."

"Yes." She sighed. If only . . . Resolutely she shook off the wistful, half-formed thought and turned her attention to the business at hand. "What can I do for you, Roger?"

"You can hear the Baby Jay case," he said with a smile. "I wanted to tell you personally instead of sending the assignment the usual route, through the law clerks."

Candy gripped the edge of her desk. The day needed only this. "Me?"

"We intend to announce it to the press within a week or two—with your permission, of course." He waited expectantly for her to comment on her selection.

"Roger, I don't know what to say." Hardly original, but she had to say *something.* And "Oh, no!" wouldn't cut it.

Her thoughts were rioting in her head. Roger was undoubtedly expecting her to express some kind of positive emotion. A *real* judge would be salivating at the challenge to set judicial precedent, to interpret and influence the laws in this delicate area.

A real judge. That was the problem, Candy thought gloomily. She had been sworn in, she had heard cases, but in truth she was a pretender on the bench. She relished slugging it out in a courtroom battle rather than listening patiently, calmly, tediously, interminably.

The Baby Jay trial and all it entailed loomed before her. The hours of pretrial preparation, studying the ponderous tomes written by all three opposing counsel. The hours of listening during the trial itself, which promised to be an exceptionally long one. Then the hours of analysis and research afterward to support whatever opinion she chose to write.

And there she would be—bored, dissatisfied, filled with self-doubt. Her every response and reaction during the trial recorded, scrutinized, and analyzed, by both the media *and* by the legal scholars of the age. She suppressed a shudder at that truly daunting thought.

"Roger, I'm honored that I've been selected to hear the case, but Russell Reauveau has had so much more experience and—"

"That's true," Roger said, interrupting. "But the selection has been made, and the judge who is going to hear the case is you, Candy."

Because she was a woman. Because the case involved three single women suing for custody of a baby. And she also happened to be single with a baby. Candy didn't kid herself about why she'd been chosen. It was hardly a compliment to her professionally. In truth, Judge Russell Reauveau would have been the better choice, Candy thought. Reauveau would savor each and every aspect of the case, relish the briefs, the study, the research, all of which she loathed. But he was a married man without children. It was definitely reverse discrimination.

"There will be intense publicity, Candy. I'm sure you're aware of that," Roger continued. "And a lot of media attention will be focused on you. You're young, beautiful, successful—and, of course, a single woman with a child. I can almost visualize the TV movie of the case. I wonder which actress will be cast as you?"

Candy's heart skipped a beat. Actress! Intense media scrutiny! She began to see a way out, after all. "Roger, perhaps now would be the time to tell you that there are some things in my background that might not stand the glare of the media spotlight."

Roger tried not to look worried, but she knew she had him there. "What sort of things?" he asked reluctantly.

Candy tried not to gulp. She could hardly tell him about Angelynne and the truth about Tori, but there were other skeletons rattling around in the Flynn family closet. "My father, Michael—a.k.a. Mickey—Flynn is a convicted felon. He's currently serving time for car theft—no, that was the last time. I can't remember the exact charge, he's spent so much time in prison on so many different charges. He's in the state penitentiary in Utah and is due for parole shortly. And knowing my father as I do, it's inevitable he'll do something shortly after his release to get himself arrested again. That isn't going to look good in the press, Roger. Can't you just see the tabloids' big scoop? BABY JAY JUDGE'S POP A JAILBIRD. It could hurt my credibility."

Roger grimaced. "I see what you mean." And then he brightened. "But look on the positive side, Candy. You've chosen not to follow his example; you're on the other side of the law." He looked worried again. "Has he—er— ever done anything particularly notorious?"

"Not yet," Candy said dryly. "But if the chance ever arose, I'm sure he'd grab it. He has incredibly poor judgment, no impulse control or conscience or feelings for anyone but himself."

"Textbook sociopath," Roger said soberly. "That must've been tough on you growing up. Sociopaths are disastrous as parents."

"They're disastrous as human beings," amended Candy. "Why don't we hold off the press release while I consider the assignment, Roger?"

"Don't let your father's record dissuade you, Candy. The court's beyond the sins-of-the-father school of philosophy."

"The media isn't. But thanks for the opportunity, Roger. I'll consider it carefully."

Marian, Tori's practical, warmhearted baby-sitter, had exciting news for Candy when she arrived home that evening. Tori had pulled herself to a sitting position for the first time that afternoon.

"I heard her awaken from her nap and went into her room, and there she was, sitting up and looking mighty pleased with herself." Marian beamed. "Most babies don't manage that till at least six months, but Tori is so strong and smart and—"

Marian continued to rave about her small charge, but Candy hardly heard her. She'd missed another milestone in her baby's life. And in the months ahead, during the laborious Baby Jay trial, she could look forward to missing even more firsts.

Marian left, and Candy eagerly assumed care of the baby. Tori was happy to socialize. She laughed and babbled and proudly pulled herself up to sit. Candy praised and applauded her newfound skill, her heart bursting with maternal joy. Every day Tori became more of a person; every day with her became more interesting.

The doorbell rang and Candy frowned, annoyed by the intrusion. She carried Tori to the door and peered through the small window to see Nick standing on the step, holding Nichole in one arm and a large brown paper bag in the other.

Her heartbeat picked up speed as she opened the door.

The two babies grinned happily. Neither adult cracked a smile.

Nick was the first to speak. He cleared his throat, his eyes holding hers. "I know you *un*invited me to dinner, but you said that Nicki was welcome anytime, and she—uh—wanted to accept your dinner invitation. In fact, she brought the dinner." He thrust the bag at Candy. "Chinese from the House of Hunan and a can of Spaghettio's. Nicki claims the Spaghettio's."

Nicki recognized her friend from breakfast and be-gan to bounce up and down in her father's arms. She reached out her arms and grabbed a tiny fistful of Candy's blue silk blouse.

"She wants to go to you," Nick said.

Candy smiled. At Nichole. "Come here, sweetheart. Of course you can stay for dinner." She settled the toddler on her left hip and Tori on her right. "You can pick her up in an hour or so. Good-bye, Nick," she said coolly, and turned to head into the kitchen.

Nick closed the door and followed her, carrying the bag. "May I stay too?" he asked quietly.

"You want to stay for dinner? Are you sure you aren't suggesting something else?" Sarcasm laced her tone as she flung his own words back at him.

"I guess I sounded like a sanctimonious creep," he admitted.

"No." She smiled coldly. "You *are* a sanctimonious creep."

He grimaced. "All right, I deserved that. Are you going to forgive me?"

"No," Candy said succinctly.

"No!" Nichole echoed.

Candy and Nick stared at her. And then Nick broke into a huge, proud grin. "Did you hear her? She said no. She's never said it before. She's learned a new word."

"No," Nichole repeated gleefully. "No, no, no, no."

Candy laughed. It was exciting to be part of a child's development. And she'd been the first to catch this milestone! "I think she's got it down pat. Can I take the credit for teaching it to her?"

"I should've guessed that you'd be the one to teach my daughter how to say no," Nick said with a droll smile. "You've sure as hell been saying it to me long enough."

"You'd better start watching your language around her, Torchia. Unless you want a little one who swears."

"Now who's being a sanctimonious creep?" Nick put down the bag of food and curved his big hands around her hips. He moved closer, drawing Candy and both children into the circle of his arms. "Am I forgiven, Candy?"

"No," Nichole squealed proudly. "No, no!" She wriggled to get down.

Candy moved away from Nick and set the child on her feet. "I have some colored measuring cups she can play with. Shannon loves to play with them when she's visiting." She thrust Tori into his arms, then pulled out the plastic cups for Nichole. "There are some frozen peas and canned peaches Nicki can have with her

Spaghettio's." She set about preparing the child's meal, purposefully ignoring Nick.

Who was difficult to ignore. He sat down on the kitchen floor, Tori on his lap, and helped Nichole stack the different-sized cups. Candy was standing nearby at the stove when she felt his warm, rough hand encircle her ankle. He stroked his fingers lazily along her calf.

"Don't, Nick."

But the passionate catch in her voice robbed her words of their meaning. Nick smiled and slid his hand up under her skirt. "You haven't said you've forgiven me, Candy." His fingers stroked the silky, sensitive spot behind her knee, and simultaneous flashes of sensual lightning streaked through both of them.

Candy took a deep, ragged breath. His slow caresses were making her feel soft and weak. "I forgive you," she said, her voice husky and taut. And then added stubbornly, "I think. You made a valid point concerning the children, but the way you expressed it was utterly—"

"Sanctimoniously creepy?" he suggested. "I agree, Candy. And I'm sorry. Do we have to rehash it again?"

She glanced at him thoughtfully. "You've always been one to forgive and forget. I can't seem to let go that easily. I have to make my point over and over from every possible angle, to pound it in . . ."

"Which is why you're such a formidable adversary in the courtroom, Candy. You keep on fighting and never let up. But we aren't in the courtroom now."

She shook her head. "No, we aren't." And she didn't want to be his adversary.

"Nicki and Tori and I are having fun down here," he said lightly, and tugged at the hem of her dark blue skirt. "Sit down and play with us."

"Sit on the floor in my new skirt?" She feigned horror, her eyes gleaming.

Nick flashed a salacious smile. "Take your skirt off. I don't mind." He skimmed his hand audaciously to her thigh. "I can think of a few dozen lewd and lusty remarks I'd like to add, but I'll restrain myself from making them, as there are children present."

"You should restrain your hands as well as your tongue," Candy said tartly and purposefully stepped out of his range. "I'm going upstairs to change clothes."

His laughter followed her out of the kitchen and up the stairs. Candy found herself smiling, as relief and anticipation surged through her. The evening promised to make up for the less than wonderful day she'd had. Nick was here, their quarrel was over. And she loved Chinese food!

Upstairs in her bedroom, she quickly stripped off her blouse, skirt, slip, and stockings. The sound of cheerful baby voices caught her attention, and she whirled around to see Nick standing in the doorway of her room, holding both babies in his arms.

His eyes swept over her lacy ivory chemise and matching bikini panties. His mouth went dry. "I—uh . . ." His voice trailed off into silence.

Candy calmly pulled a jumpsuit of butterscotch cotton from a hanger. She wasn't about to shriek like a virginal maiden and dress in her closet. With a secret inward smile she made a seductive ballet of stepping gracefully into the jumpsuit, pulling it over her hips, thrusting her breasts forward as she slipped it over her shoulders. And then she began to button it, slowly, carefully, one by one, starting from the last button and working her way up.

Nick watched her every move, making no attempt to conceal his hunger. "I forget the reason why I came up here," he admitted huskily.

"To watch me dress?" Candy suggested sweetly with a taunting, provocative smile. She pulled her hair into a short ponytail and secured it at her nape with a brightly colored scarf.

"I'd rather watch you undress. If you were trying to seduce me by that reverse striptease, you've achieved your aim, Candace. Consider me seduced. Now, what are we going to do about it?"

She merely laughed and brushed past him.

It was one of their more unconventional dinner dates.

Tori, in her plastic infant seat, was placed in the middle of the table where she could observe the activity going on around her while serving as a centerpiece of sorts. Nichole, sitting in the high chair Candy had originally bought for Scotty and then passed along from nephew to niece as the need arose, mixed together an interesting conglomeration of spaghetti rings, tiny meatballs, peas, and peach slices in her dish, pausing occasionally from her work to take a bite or two.

Candy made conversation with both little ones as she ate her sweet and sour pork, seemingly oblivious to Nick's state of discomfiture. He was hard and taut with arousal, and he shifted uncomfortably in his chair, watching Candy, wanting her with a single-mindedness that seemed to preclude everything else. Erotic thoughts of her crowded his brain, blotting out all others. He couldn't taste his fried rice or his spring rolls; he couldn't appreciate Nicki's toddler cuteness or Tori's infant charm. All he wanted to do was finish the dinner, put the children to bed, and then . . .

He groaned. He was so hard, it was an almost painful pleasure. In his mind's eye he saw himself remove the butterscotch jumpsuit he had watched her put on; saw the sexy, feminine lingerie underneath it; and the tempting curves of her body, so enticingly concealed by her smooth silk underwear.

"Dessert?"

Candy's voice drifted into his erotic reverie. He smiled a hungry wolf's smile. "Yeah!"

She didn't pretend to misunderstand the implications of his response. "I meant something along the lines of cookies or ice cream."

"And I meant something along the lines of . . . this." He caught her around the waist and pulled her down onto his lap. Capturing her chin with one hand, he tilted her mouth to receive his kiss.

His tongue thrust boldly between her lips as he angled his mouth over hers to achieve the maximum pressure. The kiss intensified deliciously as he lured her tongue into the dark, moist hollow of his mouth. His arms tightened around her, his hands moving greedily over the long, supple length of her spine, then gliding inward and upward to her rib cage.

His hand hovered just under her breast, and then suddenly, abruptly, his mouth, his arms, his lap were empty. Flushed and trembling, Candy was headed toward the sink.

Nick stood up. It wasn't an easy feat. His body was throbbing with need. "Candy," he began thickly.

"Nick, we can't sit around necking like a couple of teenagers with the children right—"

"I know, I know. You're right, of course." He made a sound that was a combination groan and sigh. He watched Candy sponge Nichole's face and hands, then hand her a vanilla-creme cookie. "How do you feel about early bedtimes for children? Like the moment Nicki finishes that cookie?"

"Is this the man who doesn't want his child to spend a night in a crib in a room in a house that isn't hers talking?" Candy said mockingly.

"I was nervous when you called this afternoon," Nick admitted, avoiding her eyes. "I was like a drowning man grasping at a life preserver."

She arched her eyebrows. "You? Nervous? Of me?"

"Last night." He shook his head. "You know how good—how great—it was between us last night, Candy. And I had all these reservations, all these resolutions. I was determined to keep it light between us. Limit us to great sex, period. Except all I could think of all day was you. How much I wanted to be with you. How crazy I am—have always been—about you. I thought about Nichole and Tori too. About how pleasant it was with the four of us at the breakfast table this morning. My child liked you, and yours liked me. Even the nanny and you and Tori liked each other! And then you called and invited Nicki and me for dinner."

"I see. Everything seemed so smooth and so inevitable. You certainly couldn't let that happen! Your relationship with me calls for obstacles and quarrels and uncertainty. This time I wasn't providing them, so you took it upon yourself to do it."

"I regretted it from the moment you hung up on me." He raked his hand through the dark thickness of his hair. "Ah, baby, can we ever break free of our past?" He caught her hand and lifted it to his mouth, gently brushing his lips over the tips of her fingers.

"I want to, Nick," Candy whispered. "But it isn't going to be easy. And you said that you wanted things simple and easy at this stage of your life."

"I know. I thought I did." He put his arms around her and rocked her against him. "But here you are, and suddenly *simple* and *easy* sounds dull and unfulfilling." He chuckled. "And *complex* and *difficult* seems absolutely irresistible."

She drew back her head and gazed up at him, and they laughed together. And then Tori began to vocalize her displeasure, and Nicki picked up on the theme herself with a few insistent hollers. Candy and Nick drew apart and turned their attention to their children.

"I thought you said Nicki wasn't a night owl like Shannon," Candy remarked to Nick a few hours later. Nichole was on her lap and they were "reading" one of the thick toddler books Candy kept on hand for her small visitors.

Tori had been bathed and put to bed long ago. Nicki, intrigued by the spectacle of Tori having a bath, had insisted on "helping" and ended up getting bathed herself. Nick had assured Candy that his daughter would be sound asleep shortly afterward, and they'd fixed up Tori's playpen as a temporary bed. But Nichole had other ideas. She was enthralled with the books Candy had brought out for her. She sat on Candy's lap and patted and turned the pages of the books while babbling a string of syllables. When her father tried to dislodge her, the little girl let out a ferocious howl.

"She's never had any books," Nick said, standing back to stare at the pair. "I never knew babies her age liked them."

"She can take these books home with her. I'll pick up more at the bookstore." Candy stood up, holding Nichole in her arms, and began to gather up the books.

"You're not kicking us out, are you?" Nick asked, frowning.

"Nick, it's past ten. Nicki's made it quite clear that she has no intention of going to sleep here, and it's time she was in bed—her own bed, where she *will* settle down and sleep." She stifled a yawn. "And I'm tired too."

"You didn't get much sleep last night," Nick reminded her, pulling her into his arms. His body was hot and hard against hers. "Neither did I, and oh, baby, I want to spend tonight exactly the same way. Go get Tori and come home with me."

Nicki squirmed and let out a protesting squawk at being crowded between them. Candy handed him the child and deftly stepped out of his arms. "Not tonight, Nick. I need a good night's sleep in my own bed. And so do you and Nicki and Tori."

Nick heaved a resigned sigh. "It's complicated, isn't it? Carrying on an affair with two babies in tow?"

Yet another reason why they should be married, Candy thought but didn't verbalize. She responded instead with a light, "You did say that *complex* and *difficult* appeals to you."

What else could she say? He'd confessed to feeling overwhelmed about his feelings for her, and she knew from long experience what the usual antidote to that particular symptom was. To back off while the relationship was stalled in retreat or a stalemate. She'd resorted to those tactics time and again herself. She suppressed a sigh. Would their timing ever favorably coincide?

She walked him to the door. "Oh, I forgot to mention that the Baby Jay case was assigned to me today."

He stared at her. "That's a pretty momentous thing to forget to mention, Candy."

She shrugged. "I suppose so. I haven't said I'll take

it. My father's criminal record is a definite drawback, what with all the publicity this case will produce."

"Honey, nobody is going to hold your father against you."

She dropped her facade of nonchalance. "That's what Roger said. But there's more, Nick. What about Angelynne? Suppose some zealous reporter manages to link us together? Shay and Case don't even know she exists, Nick! I can't let them find out about her from the press. And then there's Tori. She—"

"You've legally adopted her, Candy. There is absolutely nothing untoward about that."

"But there is!" Candy protested. "You see, Angelynne—"

"True, she gave birth to her, but Tori's original birth certificate was sealed when you adopted her, sweetheart. I may not be a lawyer, but I know as much as the average layman about adoption. A new birth certificate is issued with the adoptive parent's name, correct?"

Candy swallowed. "Yes, but—" Oh, Lord, she thought frantically. How could she tell him the whole truth? The mention of that birth certificate, carefully concealed in the long box under her bed, sent cold chills up her spine. Should she tell him? Things were still shaky between them, and she had no idea how he'd react.

Wrong! She took a deep breath. She was fairly certain how he'd react; that's why she didn't dare risk telling him. Yet.

"I think you're using your father and Angelynne and the rest of it as a smoke screen, Candy," Nick said quietly. "If you really wanted to take this case, nothing would stand in your way. I've been observing the full force of the Candace Flynn will for years. You don't retreat from potential obstacles, you mow them down."

"You're right," she admitted glumly. "Oh, Nick, the truth is that I'm dreading it. I don't want to do it. This is the consummate judge's trial, and I'm not the consummate judge." Impulsively she grasped his arm. "Nick, what should I do?"

"I can't tell you what to do, Candy. You know you'd resent it if I tried." He smiled wryly. "We've played that scene before, kid. Remember all those times I'd try to tell you what I thought you should do and then blow up when you didn't do it?"

She nodded. "And I'd accuse you of trying to control me, of being a domineering chauvinist who thought a woman belonged only in the kitchen and the bedroom."

"You were particularly threatened if I happened to be right and my advice was on target. And I'd be particularly infuriated that you wouldn't admit it. More fireworks. Another walkout. Another breakup."

They gazed bleakly at each other. "We've wasted so much time, Nick," Candy murmured. "It hurts to think about it."

"Then let's not think about it," he said pragmatically. "Let's look at the positive side. We managed just now to avoid what would've been a surefire blowup in the past. As for the custody hearing, I'm sure you'll do whatever you feel is right for you."

Candy wasn't so sure. What *was* right for her? Hearing the Baby Jay case and writing a landmark opinion while garnering international publicity? Would she be a failure for turning it down? She couldn't abide failure, couldn't handle it. And her career was the one area of her life where she'd never failed.

The lateness of the hour finally took its toll on Nicki's good nature, and she began to grow cranky.

"You have to go, Nick," Candy said softly, standing on tiptoe to kiss his cheek. She kissed the fractious Nichole too.

"Candy, I don't want to leave you like this."

"You've overcome sexual frustration before, Nick," she said teasingly, then gave him an affectionate hug. "Don't cold showers and warm milk do the trick?" She chuckled at his exaggerated, pained expression.

If it was merely sexual frustration, he certainly would overcome the feelings raging through him, Nick silently agreed as he drove his daughter home. But there was so much more. Candy had opened up to him, confided in him, and now he had to leave her. Impatience surged through him.

He forgot that only that afternoon he'd attempted to safely distance himself from her. Instead, he wanted to explore the profound changes their relationship seemed to be undergoing.

He cast a quick glance at the baby, who was already asleep in her car seat, her curls askew, her little thumb in her mouth. He smiled at the sweet sight. And then he pictured Candy, standing in front of her door, waving good night and good-bye to him. Another sweet sight. His smile widened. Tonight was far from over.

Candy was finally beginning to drift off to sleep when she heard the sound of footsteps on the stairs. Before alarm could fully register, she heard a familiar voice whisper, "It's all right, Candy. It's me."

"Nick?" She struggled to a sitting position. The room was very dark, courtesy of her black window shades. She couldn't see a thing. "How did you get in?"

She heard the rustling sounds of clothes being removed. "I'm a security man, Candace. I know a great deal about locks. And the one on your front door is pitiful—even an amateur with a hairpin could spring it. I'm sending a man out tomorrow to install a whole new set of locks with dead bolts."

The ultrafirm mattress hardly moved under his weight as he came down beside her. He groped for her in the darkness. "Where are you, baby? Damn, it's darker than a black hole in here."

"I've been accused of being part bat because I can't tolerate the light." She laughed, her heart racing with wild, primitive excitement. She instinctively found her way to him in the blackness. He was nude, and her body reacted at once to the impact of his hard warmth. She thrust her hands into his thick hair and molded herself to him, kissing him with a force that left them both stunned.

Nick felt his control shred as a potent combination of desire and need surged through him. "I love you," he admitted huskily as he slipped the thin straps of her nightgown over her shoulders. He couldn't want her or need her this much without loving her, he knew. It had always been so. "I couldn't stand another night without you, Candy. There have been too many."

"Far too many," she agreed, wrapping herself around him. She felt as if she were on fire; her body a hot, aching void yearning to be filled with his strength, with his love. She felt his hands on her breasts, his long fingers stroking her until she quivered and moaned.

He pushed the nightgown lower, over her hips and legs, until it was gone, lost in the softness of the bed covers. Her legs flexed deeply, and she lay open and vulnerable to him. His experienced fingers sought the sensuous, humid warmth of her, teasing, pleasuring. She whimpered his name and arched her body into his, twining her arms around his neck.

With a deep, hungry sound he thrust into her, and she gasped and cried out as he moved, slowly, deeply, sheathed in her hot, velvety softness.

"I love you, Nick," she cried as tiny shudders of ecstasy rippled through her again and again. Locked together in love, the fierce, fiery currents that flowed between them burst into wave after wave of rapture in a wild, incandescent explosion of release.

Eight

The Montgomery County Courthouse's announcement that Judge Candace Flynn had been assigned to hear the Baby Jay case was duly noted and reported by the press. The only personal information mentioned was her past success as a divorce lawyer and her young age upon attaining the judgeship. The media attention remained exclusively focused on the three women seeking custody of Baby Jay, each of whom was eager to tell her side of the story to any reporter who would listen.

Candy was grateful for her anonymity. Unlike the other principals in the case, the Baby Jay trial was not the most important thing in her life. Nick and Tori and Nicki were. For the first time ever, her personal life had taken precedence over her career ambitions.

She and Nick had been together constantly over the course of the past four weeks. It had been a time of renewing their old ties to each other while forging new ones. Vigorous, vital ones. Neither doubted that they had loved each other in the past, but their aspirations had been too dissimilar, their wills too strong, the lack of communication too profound, to overcome.

Things were different this time. Each had achieved professional success, each had a child, and both were now intent on making a stable, loving home, thus eliminating a major area of conflict. Whether due to time or parenting, both were more willing to compromise, to be more tolerant, to make amends. There were fewer quarrels between them, and as each became more supportive rather than argumentative with the other, the wariness and tension that had always characterized their relationship began to dissolve.

When she was with Nick and the children, Candy relaxed; she enjoyed life as she never had before. With them she could forget the tedium and the hassles of the pretrial preparation. It was just as easy to forget that her name was potentially newsworthy. But as the month of October drew to a close, so did her peaceful, precarious anonymity.

Candy left the courthouse early in the afternoon on the first of November to take Tori to the pediatrician for a routine well-baby checkup. The doctor pronounced her a healthy, six-month-old extrovert who was a little ahead of her age in coordination and motor control. Candy glowed with pride. She committed everything the doctor said to memory to share with Nick later.

The day was clear and sunny; Tori was wide-awake and exceptionally sociable. Candy abandoned her intention of returning to the courthouse. She had nothing pressing scheduled for that afternoon. "We're going to play hooky," she announced to the baby. Tori grinned and crowed.

She drove into the Georgetown shopping district and took Tori into a baby boutique where she couldn't resist buying her a pastel blue dress, adorably smocked with bright yellow ducks. When she saw a toddler-size version of the same dress, she impulsively purchased it for Nicki. Nick was an enthusiastic amateur photographer and had snapped countless photos of the children during the past month. She visualized a picture of the two little blond girls, dressed exactly alike in the blue dresses, and smiled.

They stopped in the bookstore next, and Candy chose some special baby books for Nichole. The little girl loved to sit on her lap and "read" after dinner. It was their special activity, one that Nick was relieved to cede to Candy. Reading, one-year-old-style, was not his forte.

Candy emerged from the bookstore, carrying Tori and her packages. The sunshine was warm and bright, and the pleasant autumn breeze rustled their hair. Tori liked the feel of the wind on her face. She giggled with pleasure. Candy smiled. "It's too nice to be inside, isn't it, Tori? Shall we go for a walk? There's a special place near here where I always used to go when I was in law school."

It was the path along the C&O Canal, and it was just as beautiful and peaceful now as it had been then. Candy remembered the long walks she'd taken as a law student at the nearby university. Walking had helped her unwind from the pressures of the constant stress of studying. She'd walked this path in the throes of heartbreak, too, she recalled with a grimace.

But today she felt sheer joy. It was a beautiful day, her baby was healthy, her relationship with Nick was stronger than it had ever been. Candy walked along the path, talking to Tori, enjoying the sights and sounds of nature around her.

And then she heard what seemed to be a muffled scream. Candy stopped and stared into the wooded area beyond. She heard sounds of movement, erratic thrashing noises, and then a very definite cry for help. She froze.

She'd heard of people being attacked in the secluded area surrounding the canal and had always known to avoid the place at night. But in broad daylight, in the middle of the afternoon, with all of Georgetown just a few minutes away? She stood stock-still and stared, waiting, watching, praying that what she'd heard had been wrongly interpreted by her overactive imagination.

A girl in her late teens staggered from the bushes a short distance away, and Candy could see her torn clothing, the blood on her face and body. A millisecond later two tall, hulking youths emerged from behind and grabbed the girl. One of them clasped his hand around her mouth, and the other one punched her in the stomach. The girl crumpled like a doll, and the two dragged her back into the wooded area.

Candy stared, paralyzed with horror. Seeing the men drag the helpless girl into the overgrown bushes like two beasts intent upon feasting on their prey shocked her into immobility. Her first impulse, to run after them and demand the girl's release, was immediately stifled when Tori made a soft, cooing sound. She couldn't endanger her child! How could she possibly rescue the girl with a baby in her arms? Those men could easily overpower her, anyway; there were two of them, and they were physically bigger and stronger. But running for help would take precious time. By the time she returned with willing assistance, that poor girl might very well be—

And then inspiration struck. "Fire!" she shouted, projecting her voice like she did in the courtroom to make a certain salient point. Except she increased the volume, amazing even herself with the loudness. Tori's eyes widened, her face puckered, and she burst into startled tears.

"Fire," Candy shouted again. She'd read that fire seemed to command more response than a cry for help. She prayed that particular survey had been right. "Fire!"

Tori cried louder. Candy shouted once more.

"Hey, there's a fire! Let's get outa here!" a panicky masculine voice yelled, and Candy watched the two youths run out of the woods and dash in the opposite direction.

Clutching the wailing Tori close, Candy ran on rubbery legs to where she'd seen them drag the girl. There was a peculiar ringing in her ears, and the baby's cries seemed to echo in her head. The sight of the nude girl, lying bruised and bloody in the underbrush, made her feel faint. Forcing herself to maintain a semblance of calm, Candy knelt down in the dirt and managed to struggle out of her pale green suit jacket. She laid it over the girl, who was weeping softly.

"They're gone," Candy told her. "I'm going to get help."

The girl reached up and weakly grasped the sleeve of Candy's ecru silk blouse. "Don't leave me," she whimpered tearfully.

Candy gazed down at the frightened, trembling girl, and compassion surged through her. "I won't," she promised. "I'll keep yelling fire until someone finds us."

She hollered until she was hoarse. Though it seemed like hours, it was only a few minutes until a pair of curious students arrived to investigate the fire. Candy rushed over to enlist their aid, and within fifteen minutes the police and an ambulance were on the scene.

Tori stopped crying to watch all the activity going on around her. After receiving emergency first aid from the paramedics, the girl was taken to the hospital for treatment. Two police officers asked Candy to accompany them to the local precinct house to make a statement and give a more detailed description of the two men.

The girl who'd been attacked was a local college student, one of the policeman told Candy. They were desperately eager for information about the two assailants because a similar attack on a neighborhood resident had occurred the week before in the same area.

Candy's legal training had enhanced her eye for detail, and she was able to give an excellent description of the two. The police asked her to look through a book of mug shots, and while she was doing so, word came in that two men fitting Candy's initial description had been apprehended by a police cruiser in another part of the city. Candy was asked to stay and see if she could identify the men in a lineup.

Tori, who'd been growing increasingly fussy throughout the proceedings, suddenly had had enough. She began to howl in protest.

Candy tried to comfort the baby by pacing the floor

with her. It didn't work. Neither did rocking her while talking soothingly. She gave her a pacifier, and the baby furiously spit it out. She filled an empty bottle with water and offered it to her, but Tori rejected it out of hand.

"She's tired. She's hungry and I don't have any of her formula with me," Candy said anxiously. "I have got to get her home."

"Could you call someone to come and get her?" one of the officers tactfully suggested. "It's very important that you view this lineup as soon as possible. Without a positive ID, we might have to turn these creeps loose and . . ." His voice trailed off, leaving the obvious unsaid.

Candy thought of the girl who'd been hurt and shuddered. She couldn't bear the idea of someone else having to endure a similar fate. She had to stay, but Tori definitely needed to leave. She called Nick at the TSI office and asked him to take the baby home. It never occurred to her to turn to anyone else.

"You're *where*?" Nick asked incredulously. "At a police station?"

She nearly became unglued at the sound of his voice. Her control came close to slipping as she mumbled a brief, rather incoherent explanation of what had happened. "I'll be right there," he said, hanging up before she did.

She passed the time waiting for him by walking Tori around the precinct house. She felt as if she were trapped in a crazy, waking dream.

"Judge Flynn?"

Candy turned at the sound of the clear, female voice. She recognized the young woman as an attorney who was a fellow member of the Family Law Committee of the Montgomery County Bar Association.

"Judge Flynn, I'm Emily Winslow. We met at a Family Law Committee meeting," she said. Candy managed a polite nod of acknowledgment.

The police officers were clearly surprised to hear Candy's professional title. "She's a judge?" one of them asked in disbelief.

Candy was too distracted with Tori to pay much attention, so Emily Winslow appointed herself spokeswoman. "She's Judge Candace Flynn of the Montgomery County Family Court. She's been designated to hear the upcoming Baby Jay custody trial."

The policemen had heard of the case. And so had the reporter from a local TV station who sat slouched in the corner, waiting for a story to break. He'd listened to the police scanner, and the assault on the coed had piqued his news instincts. The beautiful young mother who'd saved the girl by ingeniously shouting fire added a definite human-interest touch to the story. But learning that she was a judge assigned to Montgomery County's "custody trial of the century" had him immediately on his feet.

"Judge Flynn, I wasn't aware that you had a kid around the same age as Baby Jay," the reporter said gleefully. "I don't think anyone in the press corps knows."

"But you undoubtedly intend to remedy that," Emily Winslow interjected caustically, making no attempt to mask her distaste for the man. "Not that it's a bit relevant to the case."

"I think it could be relevant," insisted the reporter. "For example—"

"I don't want to hear this case discussed," Candy said firmly, turning sharp green eyes on the sparring pair. Both the reporter and Emily Winslow lapsed into obedient silence.

"Candy!" Nick strode into the station house shortly afterward, tall and dark and imposing. Everybody there watched him sweep Candy into his arms and hold her close. "God, baby, are you all right? What's going on?"

Candy collapsed against him, welcoming the support of his arms. She rested her head on his chest and closed her eyes, breathing in great gulps of air. The terror she'd managed to hold at bay flooded through her, and she felt weepy and weak. "That poor girl," she said shakily as tears blurred her vision. "And I was there with Tori . . . oh, Nick, I've never been so scared in my life."

"It's all right, darling," Nick said, holding her and stroking her hair. He'd made the drive across the city in record time, his anxiety mounting as he replayed her shaken, urgent message in his head. He wasn't exactly sure what had happened, but he knew that Candy and Tori had been at risk. His big hand cupped the baby's head. She was trapped between him and her mother, wiggling like a small puppy. If anything had happened to them . . . He shook off the thought, unable to tolerate it.

"Your wife is a heroine, Mr. Flynn," the reporter piped up, sidling over to them.

"Judge Flynn isn't married," Emily Winslow informed him tartly. "There is no Mr. Flynn."

The reporter stared at Candy, locked in Nick's arms, at the infant snuggled between them. "Then who are you?" he demanded of Nick.

Nick ignored him, his whole attention focused on Candy.

She continued to cling to him, drawing on his strength, his warm, comforting presence. Slowly the backlash of fear drained away, and she began to regain her composure. She drew back slightly and gazed up at Nick with a tremulous smile. "I guess everything caught up with me at once. I'm okay now." She was more than a little embarrassed by her emotional display. She straightened her shoulders and cleared her throat. It was still sore from shouting. "If you'll take the baby home now, I'll finish up here and join you later."

"Hey, Judge, you live with him?" the reporter asked hopefully. "Is he the baby's father?"

"That's none of your damn business," Emily Winslow snapped before either Nick or Candy had a chance to reply.

"Hey, it all fits in perfectly with the mondo bizarro

Baby Jay case," said the reporter with a shrug. "A judge who's a modern single woman living with the father of her baby without bothering to marry him. I love it! All of America will love it!"

Nick glared at him. "If you print a word of that, we'll sue you for slander. We aren't living together. Furthermore, Candy adopted this child."

"Yeah?" The reporter looked interested. "So then Judge Flynn is more likely to lean toward the rights of the nurturer rather than favor any biological claims? That means she'll side with Ms. A, the one who's taken care of the kid all these months. I guess the mamas who contributed the egg and the uterus are out of luck. Right, Judge?"

Candy shot him a deadly look. "Will you kindly get lost?"

"Sure," the reporter said amiably. "I've got to file this story. I think the wire services might even pick it up. How often is the judge in a controversial trial the heroine in a crime story, huh? And I like the baby angle too." He scurried off.

Candy tensed. "Nick, the last thing I want is any personal publicity from this. I—"

He cupped her shoulders with his big hands. "Relax, honey. There's no use getting upset over it. He's going to file the story no matter what. Right now you've got other things to concentrate on."

She sighed. "You're right, I suppose."

A police officer came over to tell them that it was time for her to view the lineup. Candy handed Tori to Nick, then caught his hand and gave it a squeeze. Her eyes said everything she wanted to say but couldn't, in this public a place.

Nick responded with a squeeze and a special look of his own.

It was several hours later when she made it home. Nicki and Tori had both been fed and bathed, and both nearly jumped out of Nick's arms to greet her. She hugged them, savoring their sweet baby smells, the warmth of their chubby little bodies in soft, pink-footed pajamas.

"It's so good to hold them," she murmured softly. "After what happened today, just seeing them is an affirmation of—of—" Her voice caught, and she hugged the babies close.

"Of innocence. Of goodness," Nick finished for her. "And you especially need that after what you've been through today. I heard they've arrested and charged those two goons. The local news carried the story, including your part in it, my brave, quick-witted heroine. What happened after I left?"

"I identified the men in the lineup," said Candy, "and the girl in the hospital made a positive ID from mug shots. I stopped off to see her on my way home from the police station." She paused, shaken by the memory of the visit. "The girl—Risa is her name—was badly beaten, but she's going to be all right. Physically, that is. I don't know how she'll ever get over the mental trauma."

Nick frowned, his gaze intense. "Candy, I want you to promise me that you'll never, ever take any foolish chances like that again."

She stared at him. "You mean shouting fire to scare them off? You just finished saying that it was brave and quick-witted of me."

"It was, sweetheart. But I'm talking about your being down on that path in the first place. You shouldn't have gone walking alone there, Candace. When I think of what might've happened to you—and to Tori—I literally feel sick. If those two had chosen to grab you, there isn't a thing you could've done to stop them."

"I could yell fire," she suggested brightly.

Nick's frown turned into a fierce scowl. "Skip the false bravado, Candy. You were scared out of your wits down there at the police station, and rightly so. You took an idiotic risk— "

"Are you trying to start a fight?" She tilted her head

to gaze thoughtfully at him. "To turn your tension into anger?"

"I have every reason to be tense! And angry! You could've gotten yourself and the baby killed on the path by the canal. Am I going to have to keep you on a leash to make sure you stay out of trouble?"

Those were inflammatory words that once would have ignited a war between them. But Candy did not launch a counterattack. She understood Nick—and herself—so much better than she ever had before. While she defensively converted her hurts to anger, Nick transformed his fears to anger. And he had been afraid, terrified, for her. Because he loved her.

With a soft, secret smile she walked away from him, the babies in her arms.

"Come back here," Nick commanded. "I'm not through talking to you yet."

"Well, I'm through listening," she said with commendable sweetness. "We'll call a cease-fire for now. I'm going to play with the children."

Their temporary truce lasted until the babies were tucked into cribs, Tori in her own room, Nicki in the spare bedroom.

"Now, you're going to hear me out, Candy." Nick's hands closed around her upper arms, and he held her in place. "I have some—"

"Cease-fire's over," Candy said, taunting him provocatively. "Commence firing."

"Candace, I demand that you take me seriously. You're—"

"Oh, I do," she said, interrupting again. "I'm very, very serious about you, Nick." Her eyes flashed with challenge. And with love.

"Dammit, Candy." Nick groaned, gave up on his lecture, and pulled her into his arms. "Promise me you'll be very careful."

She melted against him. "Nick, it never occurred to me that Tori and I could possibly be in danger. I was merely taking a walk, in broad daylight in the middle of the city. I always used to walk there when I was in law school, especially when I—" She sucked in a deep breath. "When I was thinking about us . . . and the baby I lost." She'd never been able to talk with him about it, but suddenly the words came easily. "I was devastated by that, Nick. I—I don't think I ever told you how much I wanted to have that baby."

He shook his head. "No, you never did. I remember that you sounded scared to death when you called to tell me you were pregnant."

"Part of me was. But the other part was thrilled because I knew I didn't have to struggle with the decision to marry you any longer. With the baby coming, I had to do it! And I realized how much I wanted to be your wife, Nick. I had it all figured out. I'd have the baby and finish law school and then support you while you went to college. I even had names picked out for the baby—Victoria Ann for a girl and Nicholas Casey for a boy."

"I thought you hated me for making you pregnant," Nick said softly. "And by the time I was granted leave to come to you, you'd already lost the baby. You refused to have anything to do with me. You got hysterical if I even tried to touch you."

"I was afraid that touching would lead to sex, and I couldn't bear to think of making love then," she confided softly. "That's how the baby started, and there was no longer a baby. For a long time afterward I equated sex and grief."

He stroked her cheek. "To me, sex was life-affirming. Proof that our love was alive. I wanted to make you pregnant again right away. The miscarriage was a fluke. There was no reason why we couldn't have a healthy child."

"I viewed the miscarriage as my own personal failure," Candy said darkly, "and I couldn't bear to risk failing again. I constantly condemned myself for losing the baby. What kind of a woman was I? I couldn't even carry a child in my body, one of the most elemental feminine functions. I decided that maybe my mother had been right about me all along; maybe I really was worthless. And I felt guilty too. I'd had some ambivalent feelings when I found out I was pregnant, and I was sure I was being punished for those."

"And you kept all those torturous thoughts inside yourself," Nick said, his voice deep with regret. "You had no one to talk to, no one to turn to. You pushed me away, and then I was sent away, to Da Nang."

"Something in me seemed to snap," she confessed, her green eyes troubled. "I felt cold inside, I felt hard and angry and cynical. And I acted the way I felt. For years and years."

"You were protecting yourself the only way you knew how. Life with your parents didn't leave you equipped with a variety of coping skills, Candy."

She nodded her head sadly. "When you tried to get me to talk about the baby, I felt so threatened. I was terrified that I'd fall apart and never be able to put myself together again. I didn't dare let that happen."

"You're too strong for it to happen, Candy. You're a survivor. You've always managed to bend instead of breaking." He leaned down and kissed her gently. "You're tough and brave and caring. I've always admired you, Candy, but never more than now."

She gazed lovingly into his eyes. *Marry me.* The words echoed in her head so loudly that she almost thought she'd spoken them. She wanted to say it, but her innate reserve held her back, and the words went unsaid.

Nick scooped her up into his arms and carried her to the bedroom. Their lovemaking that night was both passionate and tender, hot and sweet. Urgent demands melted into generous giving. They were joined body to body, soul to soul, and their simultaneous climax was a compelling paradox of release and fulfillment.

Nick was right, Candy thought afterward, as she lay languid and replete in her lover's arms. This was life-affirming, tangible proof of loving and living. But she wanted even more. Her pulses began to race as the dream, so long and so deeply repressed, surfaced into consciousness. She wanted the ultimate evidence of their passion and love. She wanted to bear him a child. It wasn't too late, her biological clock might be ticking, but it hadn't stopped.

But first . . . Her whole body felt flushed with heat. *Will you marry me*? she silently implored. Why didn't *he* say it? But not only had Nick insisted that he wouldn't propose to her again, he'd also declared that he never intended to marry again.

What if he were content to keep their affair just that, an affair? Suppose she were to propose to him and he turned her down? Candy shivered. For if she proposed and was rejected, she knew she'd never, never try it again. She'd never love again.

"Are you cold, sweetheart?" Nick asked solicitously when she shivered again.

"Just inside me," she whispered, for the chill coursing through her had nothing to do with the temperature of the room.

"Put everything that happened this afternoon out of your mind, darling," he said soothingly, misinterpreting the source of her anxiety. "You're here with me now, Candy. You're safe, love."

"Stay with me, Nick," she whispered, and he cradled her against him, holding her tight.

"Yes, baby, I'll stay."

"I don't mean just stay here for tonight. I—I mean, move here," she blurted out. She caught her breath, her heart pounding like a jackhammer. "Don't go back to California. Sell your house out there and relocate TSI headquarters to D.C. You'd keep an office in L.A., of course, but—"

"Why don't you move out there?" Nick interjected swiftly. "Resign from the bench and set up a divorce practice in L.A. I imagine you'd give those big-bucks celebrity lawyers a run for their money."

She stared at him. She'd never once considered moving. Because in her mind, the future was clear. She and Nick would marry and live here, in the D.C. area. Where her family was, where her work was.

"I'm not a member of the bar in California," she began. "I couldn't practice law there."

"Members of one state bar can get reciprocity in another state," Nick reminded her.

"Not in California. They don't have reciprocity with any other state bars. I'd have to take the bar exam there and—" She frowned impatiently. "Nick, it's not just that. I'm sure I'd pass their exam, but what about my family? Case and Shay and my nieces and nephews are all here. I don't want to be a continent away from them."

"Honey, my family is in Detroit, but we manage to keep tabs on each other. We visit back and forth—we're just an airplane flight apart."

"But I don't want to merely keep tabs on my family. Visiting once a year or so isn't like living in the same area. Why, we've seen Shay and Adam and Case and Sharla and the children almost every weekend since we've . . ." She paused, gazing into his eyes. "Since we've gotten back together. I want Tori to know her family, to grow up playing with her cousins. I . . . want that for Nicki, too, Nick."

He held her gaze. "You want Nicki to grow up playing with Tori's cousins?"

She knew he wasn't that dense! He knew damn well what she was trying to tell him. He *knew* that she was waiting for him to propose to her. And he'd obviously decided not to do it. If she wanted him to marry her, she was going to have to do the asking.

Maybe it was only fair; maybe she owed it to him since she'd been the one who'd always said no in the past. Frustration and exasperation coursed through her. How had he managed to put her in this position? He was dominating her, controlling her. . . . And a perverse part of her admired him for it. Her strength demanded strength; she respected it, even as she railed against it.

Confused and bemused, she resorted to her usual panacea, activity. She abruptly climbed out of bed.

"Where are you going?" Nick asked, watching her move, nude, around the room.

"I have to pull down the shades. The light from that damn moon is blinding," she said, grumbling. "And there's no air in here. I need to turn on the fan."

He laughed. "That's my Candy. If she can't control the situation she's landed in, by heaven, she'll control the environment."

"We'll see who has the last laugh, *Torch*," she said sternly, although she had a strong suspicion it was going to be him, not her. She loved him too much to let pride stand in her way, and if proposing to him was the price of marrying him, she was willing to pay it.

Not tonight, though. Too much had happened today. Her feelings had run the gamut from A to Z, and she hadn't yet regained her emotional equilibrium. But soon . . . soon she would propose to him and he would accept. They would be married and spend the rest of their lives together. She would be Nicki's mother and he would be Tori's father. She was full of sweet determination as she slipped back into bed, into Nick's arms.

Nine

Several days later, as Nick was preparing to leave his office for the weekend, he was approached by the eager young reporter he'd seen at the police station. He tensed. There had been no further mention of the attack in the press. The story had not been picked up by the wire services and relayed to the national media. Candy had been relieved by the lack of attention, but the sight of the news-hungry reporter instantly roused Nick's suspicions.

"Nick Torchia?" The reporter extended his hand to shake. "I'm Kieran Kaufman, Channel 5 News. I also—er—moonlight as an investigative reporter for Cord Marshall."

Nick inwardly groaned at the mention of Marshall, a notorious Washington muckraker whose column and TV show, both of which were long on innuendo and gossip and short on facts, were produced locally and syndicated across the country. Marshall had a genius for unearthing embarrassing and/or damaging information about anyone or anything.

Nick felt a pang of apprehension ripple through him. Had Marshall found out about Candy's father and his long criminal record? If so, he wouldn't hesitate to use the information to embarrass her, Nick was positive of that. All his protective instincts surged to the fore. He glared at Kieran Kaufman, not bothering to shake the proffered hand.

"I understand that your outfit did the security work for the family-court division at the Montgomery County Courthouse," Kaufman said, dropping his hand along with any further preliminaries. "In light of your relationship with Judge Candace Flynn, I find that verrry interesting. Care to comment?"

So they hadn't unearthed Mickey Flynn and his prison record. The realization made Nick smile. "Sure, I'll comment. Judge Flynn gave the name of my security firm to the court administrator, and TSI was asked to bid on the job. We won on the basis of cost and experience. It's all on the public record and completely aboveboard."

"I know all that," Kaufman acknowledged with a nod. "But while I was asking around the courthouse, I came across a far more interesting fact. It seems that Judge Flynn took a long maternity leave when she allegedly adopted her baby. Care to comment on that?"

Nick shrugged. "Adoptive mothers are granted maternity leave. Candace took it when she adopted the baby, just as any new mother would. What's the problem there?"

"Did she take the leave before or after this *alleged* adoption?" Kaufman demanded, his eyes glowing with enthusiasm. Truly he was a man who loved his work.

"What kind of a stupid question is that?" Nick regarded the other man irritably. "She took it after, of course, when the baby came to live with her. Why would she take maternity leave before she adopted the baby?"

"Because she didn't want anyone to see her in the final stages of her pregnancy!" Kieran Kaufman's voice rose triumphantly. "It's perfectly obvious to me—Candace Flynn didn't adopt that kid; she gave birth to it and concocted the adoption story. No one at the courthouse saw Judge Flynn from the time she went on leave until she returned, after the alleged adoption. And you're in on it with her, Torchia, because you're the father, even though you haven't bothered to marry the lady judge."

Nick laughed. "You've outdone yourself with your story, Kaufman. Not even Cord Marshall is going to let that one fly. Why not sell it to a confessions magazine? You show real talent for trash fiction."

Kaufman appeared nonplussed by Nick's reaction. He stared from Nick to his notes, silent, and suddenly uncertain.

"You expected rage instead of ridicule?" Nick asked, and laughed again. "Your theory is patently absurd, you twit. Do you think Candy hid out in a nunnery during her leave? Maybe she didn't go to the courthouse, but scores of other people saw her during those months and can attest to the fact that she wasn't pregnant. Furthermore she has adoption papers."

"Oh." Kaufman looked depressed. "I guess my theory is wrong, then."

"If you weren't so stupid, I might be tempted to get mad," Nick said mildly, but there was a ferocious gleam in his dark eyes, which made the young reporter flinch. "As it is, I'll let you go with a word of warning. If you keep on making up that sort of junk, you're going to find yourself in need of the services of a security firm. Since mine is the best in the business, you'd do well not to cross me. Now beat it."

Kieran Kaufman slunk away. Nick decided not to mention the encounter to Candy. She was uptight enough about the Baby Jay trial without having to worry about trash-scrounging creeps like Kaufman. Nick grimaced. It was unnerving to think that anyone would want to discredit Candy, but her position as a judge in a newsworthy trial made her a natural target. And as much as he hated to admit it, there were secrets in her life that could hurt her if brought to light. Angelynne. Mickey Flynn.

He shook off the thought. There was no way anyone could ever know that Angelynne was really Tori's mother, even if her relationship to Candy were to be revealed.

Candy would have the adoption papers, which eliminated the name of the child's birth mother. As for Mickey Flynn . . . well, almost everyone had at least one relative they were less than proud of. Candy could hardly be held accountable for the misdeeds of her ne'er-do-well father.

Having successfully defused his worries, Nick turned his thoughts to an infinitely more pleasant topic. His wedding. Candy was going to ask him to marry her any day now; of that he was certain. There had been innumberable times during the past weeks when he'd been on the verge of proposing himself, but he'd held back. Candy had to be as sure as he that she wanted marriage, for both their sakes. For their children's sakes.

His lips curved into a dry smile. And for a stubborn, controlling woman like Candace Flynn, that meant giving her the option of asking rather than replying. It meant giving her the challenge of winning him. He knew how she thrived on challenges, how much she relished a hard-won fight. She would consider his acceptance to her proposal a personal victory. His smile broadened. He would consider it a personal triumph. But in the end, they both would win. And after all these years apart, they deserved to win.

Nick and Candy spent every moment of the weekend together, ending it with a backyard barbecue at Shay and Adam's house. Case and Sharla were there, too, and the conversation inevitably included the Flynn siblings and Nick's reminiscences about growing up in the ethnic, working-class neighborhoods of Detroit. The antics of the six lively children were a constant source of entertainment. A comfortable feeling of family prevailed, an easy camaraderie that made the day a pleasure for all.

"Have you given any more thought to telling your family about Angelynne?" Nick asked as they drove to his house later that evening. "I feel guilty keeping her a secret from them."

"You dislike secrets, I know," Candy said, shifting nervously in her seat. "I'll tell everyone everything. Soon, Nick."

He reached over to pat her knee. "Good. Don't be so anxious, sweetheart. It's not going to be hard. Everyone will understand."

She wished she could get that in writing, Candy thought, lacing her fingers with Nick's. Because she had more to reveal than Angelynne's existence to her family. *Would* Nick understand?

Lillian, Nichole's nanny, had been visiting her sister for the weekend and hadn't returned when they arrived at Nick's house. "That's odd," Nick said with a worried frown. "She said she'd be back this afternoon."

"Maybe she got caught in traffic," suggested Candy. "You know how horrible the Beltway can be since they closed two lanes for construction."

But Lillian wasn't caught in traffic. She was in the hospital. Her sister called an hour later with the bad news. Lillian had fallen from the porch and broken her leg. She'd been taken to surgery and was now in traction in the hospital's orthopedic ward. She was expected to be there for at least three weeks, and in a cast with crutches for a long time after that. It would be quite a while before she could resume her duties as a nanny to an active toddler.

Nick was aghast. Along with his personal concern for the injured woman was his fatherly concern for Nichole. "What am I going to do with Nicki while I'm at work?" he asked Candy as he paced the floor in a panic. "I have two important meetings tomorrow, which will determine whether or not we land two big government contracts. I have to be there! And what about the next several months? This is a disaster!"

"Poor Nick. Trapped in the working parent's nightmare." Candy caught his hands and drew him down on the couch with her. "I have a solution. Nicki can stay with Marian and Tori at my house during the day. I'm sure Marian won't mind. She's met Nicki; she thinks she's a darling."

"But, Candy, two babies, just nine months apart! Do you think she can manage?"

"Of course. Marian has nerves of steel."

Unfortunately Marian also had food poisoning. She called Candy the next morning from her sickbed. "Salmonellosis," she groaned into the telephone. "Probably from undercooked chicken, the doctor says. I can't possibly come over today, Candy. I've never felt worse in my life."

Candy expressed her sympathy, along with her wishes for a speedy recovery. She had the names of several backup sitters whom she'd never had to call and decided that today was hardly the time to introduce a new sitter to both Tori and Nicki. She made her decision. She would stay home with the children.

"Are you sure?" Nick asked doubtfully. "You've never had to manage both of them alone. And what about your court schedule?"

"It's clear. All I'd be doing at the courthouse today is studying the Baby Jay pretrial briefs. I certainly don't mind taking some time off from that! We'll be fine, Nick. Nicki and Tori and I are going to have a wonderful day together."

He returned at the end of the day to find Candy in the small, sunny backyard with the two babies. He watched them intently. Candy was wearing jeans, a sweatshirt, and sneakers, and her hair was pulled on top of her head in a high, short ponytail. He couldn't remember seeing her dressed like that since their early days in high school, and as she walked around the yard with Tori on her hip and Nicki's hand in hers, he thought that she still looked remarkably like the girl he'd fallen in love with so many years ago. His heart blazed with love for her.

Candy turned to see him, and her whole face lit with a smile. "There's Daddy," she said to Nichole, and the little girl started to toddle toward him, laughing excitedly. Candy followed, Tori in her arms.

Nick caught the three of them in a long, warm hug. "I love you," he said to all three of them.

"We love you," Candy said, glowing.

"Today was a revelation, Nick," she told him later as they lay in bed, her head resting comfortably on his chest, her leg tucked between his. He caressed her lazily, his big hands sweeping possessively over her.

"Tell me about it, love."

"I didn't get frazzled, I took my time with the kids, we relaxed and moved at our own pace. It was great setting our own schedule, doing what I wanted to do with them. I even tuned in and caught Angelynne on the soap while the babies napped. I had fun, Nick. I loved being at home with them."

"You'd get bored doing it every day, Candy. You'd miss the law."

"I'd miss being a lawyer, not a judge. And do you know that I'd only have to handle a few divorces a year to make as much—if not more—than I earn as a judge?"

"Sounds like you're talking about those huge, dazzling settlements you used to get in your if-you-have-to-ask-you-can't-afford-Candace-Flynn bomber days."

She smiled sleepily. "Mmm-hmm. Did I tell you that I'm staying home with the children tomorrow? Marian is still sick."

"Candy?" He stared into the inky blackness. The light-killing shades had already been drawn. "Thanks, honey . . . for helping me out, for taking care of Nicki."

"I did it for me and for them, too, Nick. It feels like we're a real family, doesn't it?" *And we will be,* she promised silently. *Soon.*

Nick left the office early the next afternoon and drove to Candy's. He reached for the key she had given him when he'd had new locks installed, then remembered that he'd forgotten to put it on his key ring. Mildly annoyed with himself for his forgetfulness, he knocked at the front door. His pulse leapt expectantly. The prospect of seeing Candy never ceased to evoke a thrill of anticipation.

The door opened, and his dark eyes widened at the

sight of the girl standing before him. She was wearing a canary-yellow leotard with matching tights, and her dark hair was pulled into a braided ponytail, secured by a yellow terry-cloth band.

"You're Angelynne!" he gasped, recognizing her at once from her pictures.

"I know," the girl returned calmly. "Who are you?"

Nick stared at her as if she were an apparition. "I'm a . . . a friend of Candy's," he said carefully. He couldn't seem to drag his eyes away from the girl. She possessed a startling, dramatic beauty—with high cheekbones; wide-set, piercing blue eyes; and a well-shaped, generous mouth. She was tall and slender and possessed an ageless quality that somehow made her look both older and younger than the nineteen years he knew her to be.

"My name is Nick Torchia," he added rather dazedly.

It was Angelynne's turn to look stunned. "You're Nick Torchia?" she squeaked. "*The* Nick Torchia? Oh, I don't believe it!" She caught his arm and half dragged him inside. "I never thought I'd ever get to meet *you*!"

Nick stood, utterly bewildered, as she walked in a small circle around him, staring him up and down, from every angle.

"You look great! Exactly how I'd imagined you," she exclaimed. "Older than in the prom picture and the yearbooks, of course, but still sexy and macho and masculine!"

He wasn't sure how to handle her enthusiasm. "Candy told you about me? About us?" he asked in amazement.

"Well, not in so many words," Angelynne admitted blithely. "She did show me her high-school yearbooks when I asked to see them, and the prom picture was in one of them."

She startled him by suddenly sliding to the floor in a complete split and proceeded to touch her forehead to her right knee and then to her left. "You know Candy, she never tells anybody about anyone else. But I found out all about you and Candy when I read her diaries." She touched her face to the floor.

"Candy kept a diary?" Nick asked, his eyes fastened on the girl. She seemed to be made of rubber, bending and stretching in ways he thought impossible for the human body.

"Lots of diaries," Angelynne affirmed from upside down, in a back bend now. "She wrote almost every day in high school and college. Only sometimes after that. There haven't been any new entries for a long time, though. I always check, every time I come here."

Nick found himself temporarily at a loss for words. Fortunately Angelynne didn't seem to require a response from him. She twisted herself into a kind of tortuous pretzel position and chattered on.

"I found her diaries when I was thirteen and read them over and over. They're in a box underneath her bed with all her other important papers. I must say, your relationship with Candy gave me hours of reading enjoyment, although it drove me crazy that you two kept breaking up. And for such stupid reasons! For years I've been wanting you to get back together and live happily ever after!" She cocked her head and stared directly into his eyes. "Are you going to? Are you back together again?"

Nick averted his eyes, feeling color stain his cheeks. This youngster knew all about Candy and him, dating back to their high-school days. He found the notion disconcerting in the extreme. "I take it that Candy doesn't know you've read her diaries?" he asked tautly.

"Of course not," Angelynne said cheerfully. "Want to read them, Nick? I'll get them for you."

"No, I don't want to read them!" Nick was appalled. "I think it's reprehensible of you to go snooping into your sister's most private thoughts." Candy would flip if she were to find out, he thought. "Where is Candy, anyway?" he asked a little desperately. "I know she's not here, or you'd hardly be boasting about spying on her!"

Angelynne chose to ignore his charge and reply to his question. "No, Candy isn't here. She took Nicki and Tori for a walk. She bought a double stroller and wanted to try it out. Candy told me that she's taking care of little Nicki for a friend. You wouldn't happen to be that friend, would you, Nick?"

"I'm Nicki's father," Nick said harshly. "And, yes, Candy has been taking care of her for me during the day. You see, Lillian, Nichole's nanny—" He broke off abruptly. "Why am I explaining this to you? It's none of your concern."

"Oh, but it is!" exclaimed Angelynne. "What an exciting update! I can see why Candy hasn't had time to write in her diaries, what with taking care of two babies *and* starting up with you again."

"Angelynne, it's ethically wrong to read another person's mail or any type of private papers without their express permission," Nick said severely while trailing her into the family room. "I want you to promise to stay out of Candy's, or I'll tell her what you've been doing."

"Ah, Nick, don't be such a stiff. It's a good thing I *did* read those diaries." Angelynne stretched out flat on her stomach and began a series of push-ups. "Sometimes it's necessary to know someone else's innermost thoughts and dreams. Take Tori's name, for instance."

Nick remembered Candy quietly, painfully confiding the names she had chosen for their baby. "She named your baby Victoria when she adopted her," he said softly.

"No, *I* named her Victoria," Angelynne said, correcting him. "I was the one who filled out the birth certificate, and I knew exactly what to call her, from reading those diaries. You see, from the moment I learned I was pregnant, I knew I was going to give the baby to Candy. It was all—well, sort of karmic, if you believe in that kind of thing. I do."

Nick gave a derisive snort. "Karma, hmm? I suppose you have your own private channeler who quotes spirits from the Stone Age too."

Angelynne cast him a withering glare. "Well, if there were ever a case for reincarnation, it would have to be you and Candy," she retorted. "Your relationship has always been dangling and unfinished, and I bet it's been going on like that for centuries. You two probably started fighting over what to paint on the cave walls, and you haven't stopped since. I hope and pray that you finally get it right in *this* lifetime." She flipped over on her back and launched a regime of sit-ups without missing a breath.

"Thank you for your good wishes," Nick said dryly, regaining his sense of humor. He and Candy, painting the cave walls? "What prompted this impromptu visit of yours?" he asked. "I know Candy wasn't expecting you."

Angelynne grasped her ankles and bent herself in half. "Candy's used to me dropping in unannounced. She doesn't mind." She bit her lower lip and furrowed her brow. "I just wish I could have come with good news instead of bad. But the name Mickey Flynn *always* means bad news for us."

"Your father?" Nick sat down on the pearl-gray sectional sofa. "He's bad news, all right. What's he done now?"

Angelynne grimaced. "He escaped from prison last night. He broke out with another prisoner who was serving a life sentence for murder."

"He escaped?" Nick shook his head and heaved an exasperated groan. "It's so typical of Michael Flynn to pull a stunt like this so close to his parole hearing."

"The warden called to warn me because Mickey Flynn had been talking of going to New York City when he made parole," Angelynne said glumly. "Apparently he saw me on TV and now he thinks I'm rich." She sprang to her feet and began to twist from side to side, her hands on her hips. "I'm scared, Nick. The warden also said that Mickey and his pal are considered armed and dangerous. I wanted to warn Candy to disappear until they're caught. Luckily I don't have any more scenes for the show this week, so I'm leaving for Florida tonight to stay in a friend's condo there. I asked Candy to come, too, but she said she couldn't. Do you think you could talk her into it, Nick?"

"I don't think Candy needs to hide out in Florida, Angelynne. Your father is an incredible bungler. He was in prison out in Utah, wasn't he? Well, he'll never make it unapprehended to the East Coast. You can count on him to screw things up for himself and whoever he happens to be around."

Angelynne frowned. "You'd better be right. I'm afraid he'll come here to get money from Candy when he doesn't find me in New York. And I don't want anything to happen to her and the baby."

"Neither do I." He stared at her. "The baby," she'd said. The child she'd given birth to and then given away. He felt a chill of foreboding. "Speaking of the baby, you'd never try to take her away from Candy, would you?" His voice was threatening, his dark eyes hard. "Candy loves that child, and I want to warn you that if you ever even think of reclaiming—"

"I'd never do such a thing!" Angelynne said hotly. "Tori was born to be Candy's baby."

He was taken aback by her vehemence. "Are you saying that you deliberately planned to get pregnant to give the child to Candy?" In view of the Baby Jay case and its twisted legacy of surrogacy, such a plan didn't seem as incredible to him as it once might have.

Angelynne sighed. "No, it wasn't planned. It's an old story. I was a total jerk and fell in love. And one fateful night . . . well, I don't have to tell you. The same thing happened to you and Candy."

A shadow crossed her face, and Nick felt a pang of remorse. He knew exactly how such things happened. And how painful it was for all concerned. "I'm sorry, I didn't mean to hurt you," he said. "Tell me about your boyfriend. Candy said he was in your acting class. . . ."

"That's what I told Candy," said Angelynne, meeting his gaze.

"Uh-oh." Nick felt a sinking sensation in his chest. "Am I about to be hit with another deep, dark Flynn family secret?"

"Not if you don't want to be. You can believe that Tori's father was a boy in my acting class if you want."

Nick sighed. "Who is Tori's father, Angelynne? The facts, not the fiction."

"Have you ever heard of Thad Griffin?"

"The director? Of course, he—good Lord, Angelynne! Surely you're not implying that Thad Griffin is the baby's father?"

"You've got it in one, Nick."

Nick tried to recall what he knew about Thad Griffin. Not a great deal, as he wasn't a devotee of gossip magazines, but he would have had to be living in another solar system not to have heard some things about the handsome and talented actor-turned-director whose reputation for filmmaking—and dalliances with beautiful women—had already made him a legend in his own time.

"But Griffin's about my age," he protested. "He's too old and way too experienced for a kid like you."

"Mmm, technically he's old enough to be my father, I guess." Angelynne walked over to sit beside Nick on the sofa. "You're old enough to be my father, too, Nick. I was born the same year that Candy lost your baby." She leaned forward and murmured conspiratorially, "Have you ever thought that maybe she *didn't* lose the baby, but *told* you that she did for her own Candy-type reasons?"

She playfully tweaked his cheek. "Surprise, Daddy. I'm your little girl."

Nick felt the color drain from his face, and his heart and stomach lurched simultaneously. He muttered an Italian incantation that he'd heard his late grandmother use many times during his childhood. It was the first time he'd ever said it himself, but somehow the occasion warranted nothing else.

"Chill out, Nick. I was only kidding!" Angelynne hopped to her feet and grinned at him.

Nick heaved a despairing groan, unsure what to believe. It was horrifying to realize that it was entirely within the realm of possibility that this exotic sprite could actually be his daughter. A Candy-type reason, Angelynne had said, and he knew exactly what she meant. Candy-type reasons were often unfathomable and impossibly steadfast. And despite her increasing openness with him and her willingness to confide in him, despite their ever-growing closeness and shared concerns, he couldn't rule out the chance that she was still secretive on a number of subjects.

On top of that realization came another: He didn't fully trust her not to hurt him again. Ashen-faced, he stared at Angelynne. "Are you our daughter? Be honest with me, Angelynne."

"Nick, I'm not your kid, honest I'm not," she said, trying to reassure him. "I was just teasing you. My parents are Rainelle and Michael Flynn. I can prove it. Wait here." She rushed out of the room and returned a few minutes later with an official-looking document, which she handed to him. "Here's my birth certificate. Candy keeps it in the box under her bed. See, I told you I was only kidding."

Nick glanced at it. Sure enough, it confirmed her parentage. He tried, but failed, to stop shaking. "Your sense of humor is truly daunting," he said between clenched teeth. "Please spare me from it in the future."

"Jeez, you're so intense! You can't even take a little joke. I can see why you and Candy strike sparks off each other—she's as wired as you. I'll tell you what I often have to tell her: Lighten up!"

Nick cast her a dour glance. "Your name is all wrong, you know. It should be Devilynne. I'm sure you managed to hold your own with a slick, smooth operator like Thad Griffin."

"Well, not exactly," Angelynne confessed. "You see, I was dumb enough to think he loved me because he told me he did, and I desperately wanted to believe him. He even went to the doctor's to get me proof that he didn't have any STDs and—"

"STDs?"

"Sexually transmitted diseases. Hey, I was a virgin, Nick. I knew all about Thad's reputation, and I didn't want to catch anything. I'm not Candace Flynn's sister for nothing, you know. She taught me a lot about protecting myself."

"Apparently not enough," Nick pointed out. "You still ended up pregnant."

Angelynne nodded with a sigh. "I guess I hoped Thad loved me enough to marry me. Like I said, I was a total jerk. He dumped me before I could tell him about the baby."

Nick felt a flash of anger on her behalf. "Griffin should be shot for messing with a little girl like you."

Angelynne looked alarmed. "That's exactly what I'd expect Candy to say. That's why I invented the boy in my acting class to be Tori's father. Candy would be hot for vengeance if she found out about Thad. She'd try to destroy him—and being a barracuda lawyer, she'd find a way to do it. I know how much Candy loves me."

"You don't still love that bastard Griffin, do you?" Nick probed, frowning at the thought.

She shrugged. "I don't know. I don't think so. I do know that he's not a family man, and I'll never tell him about Tori. Anyway, she's Candy's baby. And yours, Nick. She's the baby you two should have had a long time ago."

He was unaccountably touched by her words. "I care very much for Tori," he told her. The baby's small face flashed before his mind's eye, and he saw her big, beautiful blue eyes, her engaging toothless grin, and the deep dimple in her left cheek.

A sudden perception startled him. Didn't Thad Griffin have a similar dimple in his left cheek? He glanced sharply at Angelynne. If anyone were to learn her secret . . . He thought of sleazy Kieran Kaufman, who would love to impart such a choice morsel of gossip to his equally sleazy boss, Cord Marshall. Lord, the media uproar such a revelation would cause! It would be right up there with the Baby Jay hoopla.

The Flynns and their secrets, Nick thought grimly. Angelynne was Candy's secret, and Thad Griffin was Angelynne's secret, and Tori's parentage was both their secrets. And he was squarely in the middle, knowing all. Nick Torchia, who hated secrets!

Both started at the sound of the front door opening. "Candy's back," Angelynne exclaimed, racing to the small foyer to greet her sister.

Nick followed, still holding Angelynne's birth certificate. His face lit at the sight of Candy and the two baby girls in the cushioned double stroller. Nicki sat in the front, merrily spinning the colored wooden beads affixed to the thin safety bar. Tori was in back in a semi-reclining position.

He caught Candy around the waist and pulled her into his arms. She was wearing fitted taupe slacks and an oversize taupe cotton sweater, and the plain, almost drab color had the remarkable effect of heightening her exquisite coloring. Her body was an alluring combination of slenderness and voluptuousness, and he felt desire ribbon through him as he held her close.

Candy fought the temptation to writhe sensuously under his caressing hands. She gently disengaged herself from his embrace, her face flushed. "I—uh—see you've met Angelynne," she said, her gaze flicking from one to the other.

She seemed almost nervous, and Nick smiled, finding her inhibited behavior in front of her little sister amusing. "Yes, I met Angelynne," he agreed. "An interesting experience, to be sure."

"For me too," Angelynne added with a cheeky grin. "How was your walk, Candy?"

"We had a wonderful time," Candy said lightly, bending to lift Nichole out. "This is truly the Rolls-Royce of strollers." Having been set on her feet, the little girl took off at breakneck speed.

"I'll keep an eye on her," Angelynne offered, racing to catch up.

The moment she disappeared, Nick took Candy back

in his arms, running his hands compulsively over her, seeking, possessing her curvaceous warmth. This time Candy didn't blush and pull away. She swayed into him, wrapping her arms tightly around him.

"I missed you," he said huskily, giving her gentle, nipping love bites along the curve of her neck. "How did it go with the babies today?"

His tongue caressed her skin, and she shivered with sensuous pleasure. "I can't think when you do that," she murmured. He grinned wickedly and repeated his question.

This time she managed to answer it. "It was fine, Nick. I'm amazed at how adept I'm getting at keeping up with two."

"I'm not. You're adept at anything you set your mind to doing."

She drew back and smiled up at him. "We had fun today, Nick. I love being with them. We went to Babyland and bought the stroller, then we had lunch and came home. Nicki and Tori napped while I looked over some papers and—"

"And Angelynne arrived," Nick interjected.

"With news about Dad." Candy's smile faded. "The warden had already called to warn me, although he's convinced they're headed for New York. I'm not so sure. Dad has never been predictable—his hallmark is his inconsistent inconsistency."

A frown crossed Nick's face. "You think he'll turn up here?"

Candy laughed. "Dad make it the whole way from Utah to here? Come on, Nick, you know Mickey Flynn better than that. He'll manage to get himself and the other guy caught before they cross a state border. I told Angelynne to go to Florida if she wants, but to look upon her trip as a well-earned vacation, not as an escape from Dad. I'm staying here."

They were about to kiss when Tori issued a summons from the stroller. "The kid's got a great sense of timing," Nick said with a mock grumble. He handed

Candy Angelynne's birth certificate and leaned down to scoop up Tori in his arms. She treated him to a wide, happy grin, and he felt himself melt. "What a little charmer she is," he said, turning to Candy.

She was staring down at the paper, her eyes huge. He saw the alarm registered in them. "Is there something wrong?" he asked. And then he watched her attempt to compose her face into a mask of equanimity.

Maybe it was because he'd known her so long and so well; maybe it was because her weeks of honest and open communication had impaired her ability for evasion and deception with him. Whatever, Nick knew when she replied, "Nothing," that both her words and her halting smile were false.

"I think it's something," he said, countering. He noticed that her eyes kept straying compulsively to the birth certificate in her hand. An expert in investigative observation and analysis, he drew the inevitable conclusion. "Something to do with that birth certificate."

She felt panic clutch at her throat like a strangling hand. No, she screamed silently to herself. Not now, not yet. Not under these circumstances! It wasn't the right time, he wouldn't understand.

Nick read her expression for what it was, and a foreboding chill streaked through him. He knew that whatever she was hiding was not some triviality that could be easily dismissed. And he had to know what it was. "Give it to me, Candy," Nick ordered, holding out his right hand. Little Tori was cradled in his left arm, and she smiled contentedly at Candy.

"Nick, I was going to tell you. Honestly. But I thought —I—" She knew she was babbling, and abruptly closed her mouth.

There wasn't a trace of the cool and articulate courtroom Candace Flynn in the shaky, panicky woman who stood before him. "I want to see that birth certificate," Nick said flatly. He took the paper from her, his heart sinking in his chest. He had a terrible premonition that what Angelynne had told him earlier was going to be true, after all. That the birth certificate she'd shown him "proving" that she wasn't his child was a fake. That Angelynne Flynn was going to turn out to be his and Candy's long-lost child. And he had no idea how he was going to deal with that.

He stared at Candy, his face expressionless. Tears had begun to trickle slowly, silently, down her cheeks. He dragged his eyes from her to study the paper, and his apprehension slowly turned to bewilderment. The birth certificate was notarized and valid, unmistakably stating that Angelynne Flynn had been born to Rainelle and Michael Flynn nineteen years ago.

But before he could sigh with relief, he noticed that there was another piece of paper adhering to the bottom of the birth certificate. One look at Candy's face told him *this* was the paper that was causing her distress.

With shaking hands he swiftly but carefully peeled the second paper from the first.

It was a birth certificate for Victoria Ann Flynn and was dated six months ago. According to the document, which was notarized and recorded in the state of California's Bureau of Vital Statistics, Victoria Ann Flynn's mother was . . . Candace Flynn? And her father was . . . *Nicholas Torchia*?

Ten

Tori made a cooing sound, and he stared down at her blindly. She crowed with pleasure and beamed at him. The State of California believed this baby to be his child. His and Candy's. His dark, troubled eyes flew to her face.

She was crying. He felt himself softening at the sight of her tears. Candy, who never cried, was trying to choke back sobs as the tears streamed down her cheeks. But he forced himself to remain where he was, several feet away from her. She had deceived him, he reminded himself sternly. She should have told him, could have told him, but had elected not to. The expression on his face hardened.

Candy watched his silent withdrawal and despair engulfed her. She knew that the wonderful little world she and Nick had created for themselves was ending. And that their breakup was going to be painful and bitter, as all their breakups invariably were. There was one major difference, though. This time she didn't think she had the strength or the incentive to get over it and go on.

"Nick, I wanted to tell you," she whispered, "but I didn't know how. The time never seemed to be right and—"

"And so you chose not to," he finished for her. "It was so much easier for you to keep secrets from me than to trust me with them. So much easier for you to be in control that way."

Angelynne chose that moment to join them, with a grinning Nichole. The toddler let out a squeal of pleasure as she made a sudden lurch to launch herself into Candy's arms. Candy expertly caught the child and settled her on her hip.

"Nicki's a little acrobat," Angelynne said gaily. "Or maybe a little monkey, I haven't decided which." And then she noticed that neither her sister nor Nick were smiling, that all their attention was focused on the paper in Nick's hand. "What's that?" she asked, moving closer to see.

Nick thrust the document in front of her, and she stared at it, aghast. "Oh, Candy I didn't know," she cried, whirling around to face her sister. "I grabbed my birth certificate, but I didn't know I had Tori's too. I thought you were going to put it—" She abruptly lapsed into silence.

"Where were you going to put it, Candy?" Nick demanded.

"In my safety-deposit box," Candy confessed softly.

"Where it could never be accidentally discovered," Nick said tersely. Angelynne's earlier statement suddenly sprang to mind: "I was the one who filled out the birth certificate," she'd said. "You deliberately falsified this record," he said accusingly to the girl, then turned his fierce black eyes back on Candy. "But your complicity is undeniable."

"And unforgivable?" Candy whispered sadly.

"It's all my fault, Nick," Angelynne piped up anxiously. "I registered myself at the hospital as Candace Flynn. I told you that Tori was the baby you and Candy should have had. And I fixed it so that she is."

"Angelynne saw an old picture of us together, the one taken at the senior prom, and she remembered your name," Candy explained, her voice choked with tears. "I was floored when she told me that she'd listed you as the father."

"I'm not," Nick said, glowering at Angelynne. Candy didn't know that her devious little sister had read every word in her diaries, and though he was tempted to tell her, he couldn't bring himself to do anything to strain the deep bond between the sisters.

And then an unsettling thought struck him. "There are no adoption papers, are there, Candace?" He remembered how he'd offered them as proof against Kaufman's nasty story, and he nearly groaned aloud. Suppose Kaufman decided to look up those papers? He wouldn't find them because they didn't exist. "Because you didn't legally adopt Tori, did you?"

"Not officially. Not through the courts," Candy said, confirming his grim supposition. "I—I didn't have to."

"That's the beauty of my plan," Angelynne put in ingenuously. "No adoption agency or papers or court dates. In the eyes of the law, Candy gave birth to Tori."

"And I'm her father in the eyes of the law," Nick added, his anger continuing to mount. "This birth certificate makes me legally responsible for the child until she reaches the age of eighteen." And was confirmation of Kaufman's slanderous theory. According to public record, Candy had given birth to his child out of wedlock.

Angelynne nodded her agreement. "No other man can ever try to claim her as his baby."

Had Thad Griffin ever suspected Angelynne's pregnancy? The possibility penetrated the cold rage which gripped Nick. If so, she had taken it upon herself to keep Griffin from asserting paternity forever, by negating the existence of Angelynne Flynn and Thad Griffin's child. There were no records of any such birth. The blue-eyed, dimpled baby who existed in the eyes of the law had been born to Candace Flynn and Nick Torchia. Each lie another link in the chain of their conspiracy.

"Very clever." Nick snarled softly. "And very tidy for

both you Flynns. But what about me? Don't you think I deserved to know that I was being named this child's father? And what about Tori? What do you intend to tell her when she gets older? Are you going to show her this birth certificate? This phony—this piece of perjury—"

"Tori is an infant," Candy said, interrupting. The numbing shock of pain was beginning to subside. "I haven't decided what, or how to tell her yet."

As she began to collect her wits and her shattered emotions, all her old defenses immediately began falling into place. Her tears stopped and her trembling ceased. The wretched feelings of helplessness and hopelessness were replaced by a tough, aggressive strength that propelled her to attack, instead of withdraw. Nick was right; she was ultimately a survivor whose fighting spirit would not be vanquished. Her green eyes flashed with emerald fire, and she straightened her shoulders and held her head high.

"I'm sorry you had to learn about the birth certificate this way, Nick, but you forced the issue. I had planned to tell you, but—"

"When?" Nick cut in furiously. This imperious, bellicose side of Candy had never ceased to infuriate him. His pride, as ferocious as hers, surfaced and became inseparable from his anger. *She* was in the wrong, yet had the colossal nerve to try to put *him* on the defensive?

"When did you plan to tell me, Candy?" he repeated. "After you talked me into marrying you? Oh, yes, I know that you've been aiming for a wedding ring, baby. For the first time ever, you've been panting to marry me. You've been on the verge of proposing to me, Candace, and we both know it."

Candy flinched. "What are you trying to say, Nick?"

"What do you think I'm trying to say, Candy?"

Scared, insecure, and sick with pain, she made her interpretation from that mind-set. "You've been waiting for me to propose to you so you could turn me down?" It was her worst nightmare come true. "As revenge for all those times I said no to your proposals?"

She stared at him, stricken, as unbearable waves of pain, mixed with humiliation, washed over her. She was so in love with him. Had he really set her up to cruelly, ruthlessly bring her down? Just as swiftly, every self-protective instinct she possessed rose furiously to the fore.

"You'll never get the chance to turn down my proposal, Nick Torchia," she promised, her voice shaking with the force of her emotions, "because I'll never make one. And I'll never marry you, not even if you were to get down on your knees and beg me."

"The days of me begging you for anything are gone, Candace," Nick said with quiet conviction.

"That's fortunate for you, because I have nothing to give to you, not anymore. Not ever. I never want to see you again, Nick Torchia."

Angelynne groaned. "Not this fight again!" she muttered. "It's all so predictable. Next Nick will go slamming out and— "

"What are you talking about, Angelynne?" Candy interrupted, pacing back and forth in restless agitation.

"Just another Flynn family secret," Nick replied with a glare at Angelynne. "Furthermore, our fights aren't *that* predictable!"

Still, after being told that Candy never wanted to see him again, there wasn't much else to do but go. "Nichole and I will leave now," he said stiffly. He glanced down at Tori, who was nestled comfortably in the crook of his arm. He was loath to give her up.

Candy stopped pacing, and her arms tightened around Nichole. She'd grown so attached to the baby that she couldn't bear the thought of handing her over to Nick, who planned to take the child out of her life forever! As things stood, she had no legal right ever to see Nichole Torchia again. Any judge in the land—even herself— would *have* to award her solely to her father.

Unless the judge never had the chance to rule. Candy's eyes glinted with sudden inspiration. Back in her "bomber" days, when she'd regularly blown away her opposition, she'd won many a case without ever setting foot in the courtroom. The other side would give in to her because she was a genius when it came to twisting facts to her side's advantage, because she wasn't afraid to be outrageous in her quest for victory.

This situation clearly called for a revival of her old skills. She couldn't face the thought of never seeing Nichole again. She simply couldn't give up and give her up. Nichole needed her, just as Tori needed Nick.

"I'll let you take Nichole now, but I want her to spend the day with me tomorrow," she announced boldly.

"No," Nick said at once. "I won't let you use my daughter to get to me."

Candy arched her brows. "Don't flatter yourself, Nick. Nicki and I love each other, and that has nothing to do with you. I intend to keep seeing her."

"Candy, I refuse to allow my child to be used as a weapon in this war between us."

"You'll grant me visitation rights," Candy predicted silkily.

He stared sharply at her. "Or?" he prompted. "I picked up the underlying threat, Counselor. I'll let you see Nichole or you'll do what?"

"Or I'll nail you for child-support payments," Candy returned, her voice as smooth and lethal as a double-edged stiletto. "Your name is right here on this birth certificate as Tori's father. The courts are cracking down on fathers who don't contribute to the support of their children. The fact that you haven't given so much as a dime since she's been born will weigh heavily against you. You'll be socked with back support payments, too—and with interest!"

"Candy!" Angelynne gasped, turning horrified blue eyes from her sister to Nick. "You can't make a threat like that!"

"No, she shouldn't," Nick agreed coolly. He and Angelynne both knew one pertinent fact that Candy did not.

"Well, I'm making it, and I'm prepared to follow through," Candy assured them.

"Ohhh!" A distraught Angelynne clapped her hands to her face.

Oddly Nick was beginning to enjoy himself. His initial fury had faded, and it was always stimulating to match wits with Candy. "So this is how a barracuda lawyer operates? I must admit, I'm impressed, Candace. No wonder you've racked up so many wins in your career. There must've been countless times when the other side folded from sheer incredulity at your outrageousness."

Candy ignored his taunting. When she was immersed in the intimidation process, she was impervious to mockery, threats, or insults. "Think it over, Nick. And after you have, I'm sure you'll decide to drop Nichole here tomorrow morning on your way to work."

"You're taking another day off?"

She nodded. "Marian is still sick. I have a marvelous day planned for Tori and Nicki and me."

"You'll be hearing from me, Candace," he promised. "But it may not be what you're expecting to hear."

"I have every intention of winning, *darling*," Candy said with a confidence bordering on arrogance.

"Oh, Candy!" Angelynne heaved a despairing groan.

"You're going to find me a formidable opponent, *darling*," Nick said, matching Candy's tone. "I have no intention of knuckling under to your threats, however brashly you make them."

Candy ignored him and turned her full attention to little Nichole. She kissed the baby's soft pink cheek and murmured, "Good-bye, sweetheart. I'll see you tomorrow."

Nick was astonished by the abrupt transformation. She'd gone from hard-hitting legal threats to maternal warmth without batting an eye. Even her appearance had somehow altered with her change in behavior. The cold-eyed harridan who maddened him had been replaced by a sweet-faced woman who radiated loving tenderness.

Toward Nichole, not him. There were no sweet, loving smiles for him as she reluctantly handed Nicki back to him. The little girl wanted to stay where she was and had no qualms about voicing her displeasure. She hung on to Candy's neck and began to howl. Tori was more accepting of the exchange and went to her mother's arms without protest.

Candy and Angelynne watched Nick stride from the house.

"Candy," Angelynne said nervously, "about that threat you made to Nick." She sucked in her breath. "Candy, there's something you don't know about Tori. But Nick does. It's about her father. Remember I told you that he was a boy in my acting class . . ."

Nick called later that evening.

"Have you been in touch with the Hollywood playboy yet?" Candy demanded the moment he said hello.

"Ah, boldly assuming the offensive again, I see. Well, why not? You have nothing to lose. I take it Angelynne told you about her and Griffin?"

"She told me."

"And have you set the wheels of vengeance in motion yet?"

She flashed a pseudo-smile, the likes of which had been known to reduce opposing counsel to stammering. "Did you know that one of my clients whom I represented in a nasty divorce and an even nastier custody case a few years ago happens to be an IRS agent? I won both cases for him, and we've stayed in touch. Suppose I were to call him to say I've heard rumors that something isn't quite right with Thad Griffin's income-tax returns? I'm sure that the conscientious agent would consider a tax audit, don't you?"

"And you're hoping that he'll find something amiss?"

"That would be wonderful, of course, but even if nothing turns up, I'll have the satisfaction of knowing that the lecherous creep has had to endure the inconvenience and the blind fear of a tax audit. And that's only the beginning of what I have in store for that good-for-nothing rat, Griffin."

"I almost feel sorry for the poor sucker," said Nick. "Being at the top of your hit list isn't an enviable position."

"That monster doesn't deserve any sympathy from anyone. He seduced and abandoned my baby sister. Angelynne was so young and innocent, and he used her and then threw her away like so much trash. But Griffin's going to pay and pay and pay. Oh, I'm going to make sure of that! And he'll never know why his life has suddenly taken a horrible turn for the worse!"

"Aren't you afraid that you're giving away your game plan to the enemy, Candace? Who's to say that I didn't call Griffin and that the two of us aren't in league against you and Angelynne?"

Candy paused. "You wouldn't do that to us, Nick."

"And why shouldn't I? You told me you intended to drag me into court and hit me up for child-support payments. Why shouldn't I retaliate in kind?"

"I have to see Nichole, Nick," Candy said softly. "I just couldn't let you take her out of my life forever. You know I had no intention of wringing money out of you."

Nick knew. It went against her grain to ask anyone for money, no doubt a reaction from her father's continual begging, borrowing, and stealing. He'd had to force her to take money from him that one time, years ago, to buy her prom dress, and she'd insisted on paying it back as soon as possible. Therein lay the beauty of his revenge. He smiled.

"You did make a valid point, though, Candy. My name is on that birth certificate, and legally I am Tori's father. Therefore I ought to be contributing to her support. I intend to begin doing so at once. I'll mail you a check tomorrow morning and continue to make monthly payments."

"What?" spluttered Candy.

"I also demand visitation rights, and you'll adhere to any schedule I set. Should I decide that I want my child living in the same state as her sister and I, you'll move her to California. You'll do whatever I say from here on in because I know every one of your secrets, from Angelynne to the perjured birth certificate. Finally . . finally I'm holding all the cards, Candy. I've trumped your—"

"I hate card metaphors as much as I hate card games," Candy said, interrupting crossly. "Kindly make your point without them."

"As you wish, my love. Music has always played an important part in our relationship, so I'll do it in song titles. There's a Rolling Stones song—"

"I hate the Rolling Stones," Candy said, cutting in.

He laughed, surprised that he found himself admiring rather than resenting her fighting spirit. "And you're really going to hate the song that describes your current position, Candy. 'Under My Thumb.' That's right where I have you."

Outraged, she slammed down the receiver.

Nick was exceptionally cheerful when he dropped off Nichole in the morning. "How's Daddy's little sweetheart?" he asked of Tori, cuddling her. "She's Daddy's little girl," he added with a paternal smile, watching Candy glower at him. "Legally."

He was warm and friendly toward Angelynne. "I'm looking forward to seeing a lot more of you in the future, honey," he said, draping a brotherly arm around her shoulder. "We're going to get to know each other better, and you're finally going to be introduced to your brother Case and sister Shay and their families." His dark eyes gleamed as he caught and raised Candy's hand to his mouth. "Just as soon as I say so. Isn't that right, Candy?"

Candy jerked her hand away, her skin burning from the touch of his lips. She would not react to his blatant provocations, she pledged. He was deliberately trying to make her fly off the handle, and she would *not* give him that satisfaction.

Nick began to hum a song. "Do you know this song, Angelynne?" He hummed a few more bars. "The Rolling Stones sang it."

" 'Under My Thumb'?" guessed Angelynne.

Nick looked pleased. "That's exactly right." He looked at Candy and grinned. She gave a disdainful sniff and turned away.

"Uh-oh," said Angelynne, glancing from one to the other. "I think it's a good thing I'm leaving for Florida this morning. I don't want to get caught in the crossfire." She put her arms around Nick's neck and kissed him good-bye. "Don't drag this stupid fight out too much longer," she advised in a whisper.

She gave Candy the same advice when her older sister drove her to the airport later that morning. "You really don't have any grounds for staying mad at him, Candy," she said. "He's willing to be Tori's father. He even wants to give you money for her. That's a whole lot more than her real father would have done. What else do you want from the guy?"

"I want to get out from under his thumb," Candy muttered.

"And you want him to marry you," Angelynne added, studying her sister curiously. "Were you really on the verge of proposing to him, Candy? Like he said you were?"

Candy cast a quick glance to the backseat, where Tori and Nicki were sitting in their car seats, both lulled by the rhythm of the drive. "Angelynne, I'd really rather not talk about it. Tell me about next week's script for the show. How do you think your character and her boyfriend will get out of the meat freezer that the villain locked them up in?"

"Candy, you and Nick are much more interesting than Kimberly and Billy getting out of the meat freezer. Ask Nick to marry you. You know you love him, you always have. And he loves you."

"He loves me so much that he was waiting for me to propose so he could reject me as revenge," Candy blurted out, her voice laced with the pain she'd been trying so hard to suppress.

"I didn't hear him say that—*you* were the one who said it," Angelynne insisted. "Sure he was mad at you, Candy, but he had a right to be, didn't he? That doesn't mean that he's been plotting your downfall all this time. He loves you too much to do that, trust me. Trust him!"

Candy swung the car into the lane in front of the airline terminal. "You're sweet to try to help, Angelynne," she said softly. She leaned across the seat and hugged her. "Have a wonderful time in Florida, and don't worry about me—or about our father."

Angelynne squeezed her hard and then hopped out of the car.

All during the drive back to Montgomery County from the airport, Candy thought about her conversation with Angelynne. "Trust him," she'd said. "Ask him to marry you, you know you love him, you always have. And he loves you too." How strange to have her little sister give her advice. It was a definite role reversal. Even stranger, she was tempted to take Angelynne's advice. To trust Nick. To believe that he loved her and wouldn't plot some elaborate revenge to hurt her.

As her sister had pointed out, Nick hadn't said that he'd been waiting for her to propose so he could turn her down. That had been a vintage Candace Flynn conclusion. Has she been projecting her own penchant for vengeance onto him?

She thought about his infuriating phone call the night before, in which he'd matched her threat for threat and even outwitted her. She thought about his maddening taunts about having her "under his thumb." Hadn't she invited that sort of retaliation by alleging that she planned to take him to court for child support? Her lips curved into a reluctant smile. She'd made a ridiculous, outrageous threat, and he'd called her bluff and come up with an even better one. Suddenly the whole quarrel struck her as absurd.

She should have told him about Tori's birth certificate, she admitted to herself. Nick did have a right to be angry that she hadn't. But he hadn't been angry when he'd come to the house with Nicki today. He'd been in an extraordinarily good mood, and his teasing had definitely held an element of sexual provocation. A hot, sensual knot of tension began to throb deep inside her, and her heart began to thud in matching rhythm.

The anger and confusion that had clouded her judgment slowly lifted. Nick had made it perfectly clear he was going to be a permanent part of her life by citing his "legal" relationship with Tori. He'd brought Nichole to her today when she had asked him to. She knew he wouldn't let her continue to be involved with his child, nor would he sustain a relationship with her child if he didn't intend for the four of them to be together.

Suddenly it all seemed so easy. When Nick came home that day, she was going to throw all pride and caution to the wind and propose. And then she would call Case and Shay with the good news and tell them the full story of Angelynne. At long last there would be no more secrets, nothing to hide.

She felt lighter than air. Why hadn't she done this weeks ago? she wondered, then another inspiration struck. While she was finally setting her personal life to rights, why not make a stab for professional happiness too? It was time to shed her black robe and gavel and judgely dispassion and get back to the slings and arrows, the challenges and machinations of a first-class divorce practice. Life was too short to waste in a job she detested, when the career she loved was available. And she could handle as many or as few cases as she chose, fitting her schedule according to the children's ages and needs.

She decided to go to the courthouse immediately and submit her resignation. What was the point of waiting when she knew what needed to be done? Characteristically, having decided on a course of action, she was resolute in her determination to follow through.

She carried Tori and Nicki into her office, passing her law clerk, Jack Conrad, in the hall. He appeared stunned to see her in soft pink velour rather than in her formidable judicial robes. Nor did he seem to be as afraid of her in her mother persona, Candy noted with amusement. Perhaps the sight of the two babies in her arms rendered her more innocuous in his eyes.

Her secretary wasn't in sight, so she put the babies on the rug and wrote up her letter of resignation, citing personal reasons for her departure. Then she placed it on Sally's desk, to be typed and delivered to the court administrator. Her only regret was that she hadn't done it sooner. Judge Russell Reauveau probably would be assigned to take the Baby Jay case, and she wished him well with it.

There was no one around as she carried the babies back to the car. The next time she was in the courtroom, she would be appearing before a judge, not serving as one. The thought made her smile with satisfaction and anticipation. She felt as if she'd been sprung from a trap.

Nichole and Tori fell asleep in their car seats as she drove along the highway. Candy's thoughts were full of Nick. She couldn't wait to see him tonight, couldn't wait to have everything resolved between them. Why should she wait? she thought suddenly. She could drive to his office right now. The children were sleeping, she was near the Beltway, and it was less than an hour's drive from the TSI offices.

Fifteen minutes later she knew she'd made a drastic mistake. There was a record-breaking traffic jam on the Beltway. All traffic came to a dead stop. After a while the drivers and passengers began to leave their vehicles to walk around and commiserate. Candy glanced back at the babies, who were still asleep, then climbed out of her car and asked the trucker in front of her if he knew anything about the delay.

The news from his CB radio was bad. "We're going to be stuck here a long, long time," the trucker said glumly. "There's been a six car pileup a few miles ahead. A tractor-trailer overturned and is lying on its side across the road. You add all that to the freakin' construction that's closed two lanes and we've got a helluva wait."

Candy returned to her car in disgust. She rolled down all the windows and waited for Tori and Nicki to wake up. When they did, they weren't at all pleased to be stuck in the car without food or drink. Candy tried to force herself to stay calm. But she had only one diaper apiece for each baby. If they were here for hours. . .

Eleven

The call to the TSI office was tense. "There's big trouble at the Montgomery Courthouse," one of Nick's security agents reported to him. "Two escaped cons shot their way inside and wounded a bailiff. Word has it they're holed up in a judge's chambers and have taken several hostages, including the judge."

Nick silently uttered a thankful prayer that Candy hadn't gone to the courthouse today. "I'll send a team right out," he told the agent.

The county sheriff's office called next, requesting TSI's presence at the scene. Nick assured them that they were on their way. "Don't go near the Beltway," the officer advised. "There's a monster traffic jam. From what we hear, nobody's gonna get out of it for hours."

Taking a longer route that circumvented the Beltway, Nick arrived to find the courthouse in chaos. County and state police were on the scene, along with local television camera crews and an increasing number of onlookers. Anthony Tesone, the court administrator, was frantic.

"You suggested installing metal detectors in the main entrance, but we vetoed it as too impractical and expensive," Tesone said to Nick. "The family courtrooms are secure, but these two creeps didn't go near a courtroom. They walked right into the building and headed toward the judges' chambers. One of the bailiffs thought they were acting peculiar and stopped them. That's when he was shot."

"Killed?" Nick asked tersely.

"Shot in the shoulder," replied a policeman. "He's been taken to the hospital. Fortunately he wasn't seriously hurt."

"I heard there were hostages," one of Nick's agents interjected, and the sheriff nodded grimly.

"According to eyewitnesses, after they shot the bailiff, they grabbed a couple of people who were standing in the corridor and dragged them into one of the judge's chambers. A law clerk had seen the judge enter earlier and didn't see her leave. We're assuming that she's being held too."

Nick arched his brows. "She?" he asked. He knew Candy was safe at home, but that knowledge didn't stop a chill of fear from shooting through him.

"Flynn. Judge Flynn," the sheriff said. "Here's the really lousy part. According to the clerk, she wasn't even supposed to be in today. She stopped by her office with her two little kids, and no one saw them leave. We're assuming the gunmen have them."

"You mean the kids are in there too?" A reporter had joined them.

The sheriff frowned. "As far as we know. We're trying to set up telephone contact with the two men to find out who the hell they are and what they want."

Nick barely heard him. The news had affected him like a massive blow to the skull. The color drained from his face, and he felt as if he were going to fall. Candy and the children were being held hostage by two gunmen? He went hot and cold at the same time. From that moment on, he functioned mechanically, without being aware of what he was doing or saying.

He couldn't stop the coldness that spread through him all the way to his soul. Candy and the babies were in grave danger, his mind screamed, and there was nothing he could do to protect them. His stomach rolled, every nerve and muscle in his body was drawn as tight as a bowstring. Candy. Nicki. Tori. His woman, his love, his little girls. What would he do if—

"They've called Judge Flynn's office and have one of the guys on the phone," a police officer called to them. "We've got some information on the escaped cons. They broke out of the state pen in Utah—"

"Utah?" Nick echoed. Oh, God, it couldn't possibly be Mickey Flynn and the *convicted murderer* who'd escaped with him. Could it?

"They've been traced through a string of stolen cars and robberies from Utah to here," the policeman continued. "Apparently they dumped one car and stole a new one in every city they've passed through—Salt Lake City, Denver, Kansas City, St. Louis, Cincinnati, and Pittsburgh. They've knocked over a bunch of convenience stores and gas stations along the way, randomly shooting whoever happened to get in their way. They've practically left a Day-Glo trail. Wonder why in the hell they ended up here in the courthouse, of all places?"

"Have there been any fatalities when they were on the run?" a reporter asked.

"None reported. By some miracle, they've only wounded their victims."

"Maybe they're the duo who couldn't shoot straight," offered another reporter. A few laughed at the macabre humor.

Nick felt physically ill. "Do you have their names yet?" he asked in a taut voice he scarcely recognized as his own.

"Yeah, one is named Scali. He's serving a life sentence for killing a bank teller during an attempted robbery. The other guy was serving six to ten for assault. His name is Flynn."

"Same name as the judge," a reporter noted absently.

Nick abruptly turned and made his way to the phones, where a member of a SWAT team, which had been summoned from the city, was talking to the convicts inside the judge's chambers. "I know one of the guys. Let me talk to him," he demanded.

The phone was handed to him. "Mickey, this is Nick Torchia, from the old neighborhood in Detroit."

"Case and Candy's friend?" Mickey said with his usual superficial conviviality. "How's your mother, kid? Still got the store on the corner?"

Talking to Mickey Flynn was as useless and enraging as it had been all those years ago in Detroit, Nick thought as impotent fury raged through him. Flynn refused to let him talk to Candy; he refused to say if she and the children and the other hostages were all right. He stated that he and his companion would release the hostages when and if they were given a plane and flown to Rio de Janeiro. "Otherwise we'll have to blow 'em all away, Nick," Mickey said cheerfully.

Candy and hundreds of others remained mired in the most massive traffic jam in the history of the Beltway. Everybody left their cars and milled around the highway, exchanging information and complaints. An atmosphere of esprit de corps prevailed. Sympathetic motorists took pity on Candy and the two howling babies and managed to scrounge up something for the hungry children to eat. Nicki had her first candy bar, compliments of a salesman in a blue Oldsmobile. Tori had her first cookie, from a vacationing family's stash of Lorna Doones. There were plenty of cupcakes, thanks to a generous housewife who'd been on her way to deliver treats to her son's elementary-school class. Someone else gave Candy a can of ginger ale to pour into the babies' empty bottles. Stuffed with cookies, candy, cake, and soda pop, the two little ones were content to let Candy carry them around outdoors until they grew sleepy and were returned to the car for a nap.

Four hours later the trucker with the CB advised everyone to get ready to go. "They've cleared the road and are starting to let the cars three miles ahead of us move," he announced. There was a round of cheers and applause.

At last the traffic began to flow again. Candy abandoned her plan of going to Nick's office. She had to get the babies home, and he would be back soon, anyway. Switching on the radio, she began to think about how, when, and where she would propose to Nick. A news bulletin cut into the song that was playing. She listened—and then gasped in horror.

There was a hostage situation at the Montgomery County Courthouse! Two gunmen were holding an unknown number of people, *including one of the family court judges,* in a judge's chambers!

"Oh, no!" she cried aloud. Which judge could it be? Wright? Benton? Reauveau? If it was poor old Judge Benton, he was likely to be in danger of cardiac arrest. She remembered the older man's almost obsessive worry about courtroom violence. And Roger Wright was the father of three, and Russell Reauveau—why, she had just bequeathed him the Baby Jay case four hours ago.

She drove immediately to the courthouse. She had to know what was going on, to see if she could offer any help. She thought of the hostage judge's family members and tried to imagine the dreadful state of fear they must be in.

There was a huge crowd at the courthouse, and the police weren't welcoming the curious spectators who continued to gather. But she had to do something, Candy thought determinedly. One of her colleagues, one of her friends, was in danger! Carrying both babies, she snaked through the crowd, finally making her way to a uniformed policeman.

"I'm Judge Candace Flynn," she said breathlessly, "and I—"

"My God, it's her!" the policeman gasped. "With the kids. They escaped!"

Candy stared at him, bewildered. And then came the sickening, distinct sound of two gunshots. People in the crowd screamed. The policeman grabbed Candy and dragged her toward a section near the front of the courthouse that had been cordoned off and was filled with officers dressed as if for guerrilla warfare.

Nick heard the shots and grabbed the edge of the table for support. He'd tried talking to Flynn and his cohort, tried reasoning with them. So had the officers specially trained in hostage negotiations. They'd even brought in a psychiatrist to try his hand at persuading the two men to surrender. All to no avail. And now gunshots. The SWAT team charged into the building, weapons at the ready. Candy and the children were trapped in there! Nick closed his eyes and knew that his life was over if they didn't come back to him.

"Look, she's here!"

The exultant bellow of a police officer caused every head in the special area to turn. Dazed, Nick looked in the same direction as everyone else. And saw . . . Candy carrying the babies?

He blinked, certain that he'd gone over the edge and was hallucinating. But a second and a third glance confirmed what he was afraid to let himself believe. Candy, looking more than a little confused, was being hustled through the crowd by a police officer, with Nicki and Tori in her arms.

"She did it!" the policeman shouted. "She got out!"

Nick pushed his way through the crowd, his heart thundering in his ears. "Candy!" he said in a raspy tone, and swept her into his arms. "Oh, baby, I can't believe it! I can't believe you're here. Are you all right? Are the kids all right? How did you do it?"

She wondered how they'd known she and the children had been trapped in the traffic jam. But she was too happy to be with Nick really to care. He was here and was holding her as if he'd never let go. She knew beyond a doubt that the previous day's crisis was behind them.

"We're fine, Nick," she assured him, snuggling close. "We just waited around until the traffic started moving, and then we made it out. Nicki and Tori are stuffed with junk food, though. I hope they don't get belly-aches." And then she remembered the terrible reason why she was there. "Oh, Nick, which judge is being held hostage? I came as soon as I heard. Is there anything I can do to help?"

Nick's reaction was most peculiar. She didn't know if he were laughing or crying. He didn't either. "*You* were the judge we thought was in there," he explained, holding her even tighter. "We thought Mickey and his partner had you and the kids."

Tori and Nicki began to fuss. They'd spent a long, wearing day in a traffic jam and were now being squashed between parents. Reluctantly Candy and Nick drew apart.

Only then did his words fully dawn on her. "Mickey? Oh, Nick, you can't mean that my father is one of the gunmen?"

Nick pulled her back into his arms, oblivious to the children's disgruntled yowling. "It's okay, Candy, I'm here. We're together. We can handle anything that happens as long as we're together. Remember that."

A few minutes later it was all over. The three hostages, all courthouse employees, were released unharmed. The two escapees were carried out on stretchers, both shot but neither critically wounded. One of the hostages gave the police and the news media an account of what had happened inside. Flynn and Scali had spent most of the time arguing over everything, from what kind of sandwiches to order from the hostage negotiation team to the model of plane they should demand to fly them to Rio. Eventually their argument became so heated that they'd each drawn their guns and shot each other.

It was a typical Mickey Flynn disaster, the Flynn siblings would later agree. He had been coming to demand money from Candy and had become furious and frustrated when he'd learned that she wasn't in the courthouse that day. Shooting the bailiff and taking the hostages had been unplanned, done on the spur of the moment. The two convicts were to be returned to Utah and charged with a long list of crimes that would preclude any chance of parole for either for decades to come.

Both Nick and Candy were drained when they left the courthouse. They concentrated on the children, letting themselves unwind as they played with them and bathed and fed them. It wasn't until both babies were tucked into their cribs that Candy remembered to tell Nick that she'd resigned from the bench.

And then she took a deep breath and added, "Nick, there's been something that I've been wanting to ask you for a long time. Will you please, please marry me?"

"Sweetheart, you didn't have to ask me, I intended to propose to you." His face was shadowed with remorse. "After I apologized."

"For what?"

"For yesterday. For hurting you and making you cry." His dark eyes were filled with regret. "I relived it all over and over today while I thought you were being held hostage by those lunatics, and I wanted to take back everything I'd said and done, to turn back the clock and take you in my arms and tell you how much I care. My anger seemed so inconsequential, so trivial and selfish. Candy, I love you so much, and I—"

"Nick, both Angelynne and I agreed that you had a right to be angry with us about the birth certificate," Candy cut in passionately, "and I said some pretty rotten things yesterday, too, remember? One of the worst was that I had nothing to give you anymore, when I really want to give you everything I have, everything that I am."

"Sweetheart, I said I was through begging you for anything, but that isn't true. I'm begging for your forgiveness."

"Nick, you don't have to. I—" She stopped, her eyes suddenly sparkling. "We'd better call a halt to all these mea culpas right now, Nick. I can see where this is heading. Pretty soon we're going to be arguing over who's the guiltier one, who hurt who more. You'll insist it's you, and I'll insist it's me. Let's just agree that we're both to blame and let it go at that."

His lips curved into a slow smile that lit his dark eyes. "You're very generous, Candace." He took her hand in his and led her up the stairs to the bedroom.

"So are you," she said playfully. "Generous to a fault. Offering to make those child-support payments . . ."

He carefully and deliberately removed her pink velour shirt, then hooked his thumbs under the waistband of her matching slacks and pulled them off. A sensuous shiver undulated through her.

"Do you want Tori and me to move to California?" she asked softly, closing her hand over the buckle of his belt. Her knuckles brushed over him suggestively. "I'll do anything you want, Nick. After all, you have me under your thumb."

"And you have me wrapped around your little finger," he said huskily. "Let's skip the digital metaphors, honey. I want to propose to you. Will you marry me, Candy? And live here in Montgomery County with me? We'll go house-hunting as soon as possible."

"You're too late with your proposal, Nick. I already asked you to marry me first."

"Then my answer is a resounding yes."

"So is mine. And, yes, I'd love to go house-hunting with you. Is tomorrow soon enough to start?"

"Tomorrow is perfect, my love," he murmured. They kissed, a slow, deep kiss of love and possession, of passion and commitment.

"I want to have your baby," Candy whispered, sliding her hands over his broad shoulders as she pressed herself against his hardness and warmth. Her body was ready and ripe and aching to conceive. "I don't want to wait, Nick."

He laughed softly, unfastening the clip of her pink brassiere and cupping her full breasts in his hands. "Is tonight soon enough to start?"

"Tonight is perfect, my love," she said, and they sank down onto the bed together. . . .

Exactly nine months and three days later, Candy and Nick brought Matthew Nicholas Torchia home from the hospital where he'd been born in a modern birthing room, his father at his mother's side throughout her long labor and delivery.

Nicki and Tori were waiting for their parents under Lillian's watchful eye. The two little girls were intrigued with their new brother but quickly lost interest when he continued to snooze. It was much more fun to sit together on Mommy's lap in the big rocking chair while she read a stack of new books to them.

"They missed you while you were in the hospital," Nick said, watching the trio with warm, dark eyes. "We all did, darling. Me, most of all."

Candy looked up from the storybook and smiled at him. Their eyes met and exchanged private messages of love.

"Mommy, read!" demanded Nichole imperiously. She considered herself the true boss of the family. Tori, currently an agreeable and mild-mannered toddler, was willing to go along with that.

Nick sat down on the sofa nearby and glanced idly through the newspaper. The Baby Jay trial, Judge Russell Reauveau presiding, was entering its fourth month, with no one having a clue as to how the judge would rule. It had been relegated to the back pages of the paper, not far from the weekly daytime soap-opera synopses. Nick skimmed the column, his eyes lighting on one particular paragraph.

"You'll be happy to know that Angelynne's character, Kimberly, and her intrepid boyfriend, Billy, have escaped from the clutches of the villainous kidnapper and are now on the run," he said to Candy.

"I watched every day in the hospital," Candy told him

with a grin. "I'm glad Angelynne's life is running more smoothly than poor Kimberly's."

Candy had broken the news of their half sister's existence to Case and Shay the same day she'd announced that she and Nick planned to marry. The initial meeting of all the Flynns went well. Shay and Angelynne were instantly taken with each other and had seen each other frequently during the past months. Predictably, Case had been more guarded in his response, but Sharla's warm acceptance made up for his reserve. He had already accepted Angelynne as his sister, and Candy knew that in time he would come to love her too.

Later that evening, after tucking their three children snugly into their cribs, Candy and Nick walked into the spacious family room, their arms around each other. He put a record on the turntable and drew Candy down onto his lap. As their beloved old Motown favorites resounded from the speakers, they smiled at each other, then kissed with all the passionate intensity that had always burned between them.

"We're together forever, Nick," Candy said dreamily, clinging to him.

"And beyond, my love," added Nick.

THE EDITOR'S CORNER

We sail into our LOVESWEPT summer with six couples who, at first glance, seem to be unlikely matches. What they all have in common, and the reason that everything works out in the end, is Cupid's arrow. When true love strikes, there's no turning back—not for Shawna and Parker, her fiance, who doesn't even remember that he's engaged; not for Annabella and Terry, who live in completely different worlds; not for Summer and Cabe, who can't forget their teenage love. Holly and Steven were never meant to fall in love—Holly was supposed to get a juicy story, not a marriage proposal, from the famous bachelor. And our last two couples for the month are probably the most unlikely matches of all—strangers thrown together for a night who can't resist Cupid's arrow and turn an evening of romance into a lifetime of love!

We're very pleased to introduce Susan Crose to you this month. With **THE BRASS RING,** she's making her debut as a LOVESWEPT author—and what a sparkling debut it is! Be on the lookout for the beautiful cover on this book—it's our first bride and groom in a long time!

THE BRASS RING, LOVESWEPT #264, opens on the eve of Shawna McGuire's and Parker Harrison's wedding day when it seems that nothing can mar their perfect joy and anticipation on becoming husband and wife. But there's a terrible accident, and Shawna is left waiting at the church. Shawna almost loses her man, but she never gives up, and finally they do get to say their vows. This is a story about falling in love with the same person twice, and what could be more romantic than that?

Joan Elliott Pickart's **THE ENCHANTING MISS ANNA-BELLA,** LOVESWEPT #265, is such an enchanting love story that I guarantee you won't want to put this book down. Miss Annabella is the librarian in Harmony, Oklahoma, and Terry Russell is a gorgeous, blue-eyed, ladykiller pilot who has returned to the tiny town to visit his folks. All the ladies in Harmony fantasize about handsome Terry Russell, but Annabella doesn't even know what a fantasy is! Annabella's a late bloomer, and Terry is the

(continued)

one who helps her to blossom. Terry sees the woman hidden inside, and he falls in love with her. Annabella discovers herself, and then she can return Terry's love. When that happens, it's a match made in heaven!

FLYNN'S FATE, by Patt Bucheister, LOVESWEPT #266, is another example of this author's skill in touching our emotions. Summer Roberts loves the small town life and doesn't trust Cabe Flynn, the city slicker who lives life in Chicago's fast lane. Cabe was her teenage heartthrob, but years ago he gave up on Clearview and on Summer. Now he's back to claim his legacy, and Summer finds she can't bear to spend time with him because he awakens a sweet, wild hunger in her. Cabe wants to explore the intense attraction between them; he won't ignore his growing desire. He knows his own mind, and he also knows that Summer is his destiny—and with moonlight sails and words of love, he shows her this truth.

In **MADE FOR EACH OTHER** by Doris Parmett, LOVESWEPT #267, it's our heroine Holly Anderson's job to get an exclusive interview from LA's most eligible bachelor. Steven Chadwick guards his privacy so Holly goes undercover to get the scoop. She has no problem getting to know the gorgeous millionaire—in fact, he becomes her best friend and constant companion. Steven is too wonderful for words, and too gorgeous to resist, and Holly knows she must come clean and risk ruining their relationship. When friendly hugs turn into sizzling embraces, Holly gives up her story to gain his love. Best friends become best lovers! Doris Parmett is able to juggle all the elements of this story and deliver a wonderfully entertaining read.

STRICTLY BUSINESS by Linda Cajio, LOVESWEPT #268, maybe should have been titled, "Strictly Monkey Business". That describes the opening scene where Jess Brannen and Nick Mikaris wake up in bed together scarcely having set eyes on each other before! They are both victims of a practical joke.

Things go from bad to worse when Jess shows up for a job interview and finds Nick behind the desk. They can't seem to stay away from each other, and Nick can't

(continued)

forget his image of her in that satin slip! Jess keeps insisting that she won't mix business with pleasure, even when she has the pleasure of experiencing his wildfire kisses. She doth protest too much—and finally her "no" becomes a "yes." This is Linda Cajio's sixth book for LOVESWEPT, and I know I speak for all your fans when I say, "Keep these wonderful stories coming, Linda!"

One of your favorite LOVESWEPT authors, Helen Mittermeyer, has a new book this month, and it's provocatively—and appropriately!—titled **ABLAZE**, LOVESWEPT #269. Heller Blane is a stunning blond actress working double shifts because she's desperately in need of funds. But is she desperate enough to accept $10,000 from a mysterious stranger *just* to have dinner with him? Conrad Wendell is dangerously appealing, and Heller is drawn to him. When their passionate night is over, she makes her escape, but Conrad cannot forget her. He's fallen in love with his vanished siren—she touched his soul—and he won't be happy until she's in his arms again. Thank you, Helen, for a new LOVESWEPT. **ABLAZE** has set our hearts on fire!

The HOMETOWN HUNK CONTEST is coming! We promised you entry blanks this month, but due to scheduling changes, the contest will officially begin next month. Just keep your eyes open for the magnificent men in your own hometown, then learn how to enter our HOMETOWN HUNK CONTEST *next month*.

Happy reading!

Sincerely,

Carolyn Nichols

Carolyn Nichols
   Editor
LOVESWEPT
Bantam Books
666 Fifth Avenue
New York, NY 10103

ENTER
THE DELANEYS, THE UNTAMED YEARS
MISSISSIPPI QUEEN' RIVERBOAT CRUISE
SWEEPSTAKES
W I N
7 NIGHTS ABOARD THE LUXURIOUS
MISSISSIPPI QUEEN STEAMBOAT
including double occupancy accommodations,
meals and fabulous entertainment for two

She's elegant. Regal. Alive with music and moonlight. You'll find
a Jacuzzi, gym, sauna, movie theatre, gift shop, library, beauty
salon and multi-tiered sun deck aboard...plus a splendid dining
room and lounges, beveled mirrors, polished brass, a Grand
Saloon where big band sounds soothe your soul and set your feet
to dancing! For further information and/or reservations on the
Mississippi Queen and Delta Queen* Steamboats
CALL 1-800-458-6789!

Sweepstakes travel arrangements by
RELIABLE TRAVEL INTERNATIONAL, INC.

Whether you're travelling for business, romance or adventure,
you're a winner with Reliable Travel International!
CALL TOLL FREE FOR INFORMATION AND RESERVATIONS
1-800-645-6504 Ext. 413

**MISSISSIPPI QUEEN RIVERBOAT CRUISE SWEEPSTAKES
RULES AND ENTRY FORMS ALSO APPEAR IN THE
FOLLOWING BANTAM <u>LOVESWEPT</u> NOVELS:**

THE GRAND FINALE	**MAN FROM HALF MOON BAY**
HOLD ON TIGHT	**OUTLAW DEREK**
*CONFLICT OF INTEREST	***DIVINE DESIGN**
*WARM FUZZIES	***BABY, BABY**
*FOR LOVE OF LACEY	***HAWK O'TOOLE'S HOSTAGE**

and in

**THE DELANEYS, THE UNTAMED YEARS:
COPPER FIRE; WILD SILVER; GOLDEN FLAMES**

*On sale week of May 2, 1988   SW'10

OFFICIAL DELANEYS, THE UNTAMED YEARS MISSISSIPPI QUEEN' RIVERBOAT CRUISE SWEEPSTAKES RULES

1. NO PURCHASE NECESSARY. Enter by completing the Official Entry Form below (or print your name, address, date of birth and telephone number on a plain 3" x 5" card) and send to:

Bantam Books
Delaneys, THE UNTAMED YEARS Sweepstakes
Dept. HBG
666 Fifth Avenue
New York, NY 10103

2. One Grand Prize will be awarded. There will be no prize substitutions or cash equivalents permitted. Grand Prize is a 7-night riverboat cruise for two on the luxury steamboat, The Mississippi Queen. Double occupancy accommodations, meals and on-board entertainment included. Round trip airfare provided by Reliable Travel International, Inc. (Estimated retail value $5,500.00. Exact value depends on actual point of departure.)

3. All entries must be postmarked and received by Bantam Books no later than August 1, 1988. The winner, chosen by random drawing, will be announced and notified by November 30, 1988. Trip must be completed by December 31, 1989, and is subject to space availability determined by Delta Queen Steamboat Company, and airline space availability determined by Reliable Travel International. If the Grand Prize winner is under 21 years of age on August 1, 1988, he/she must be accompanied by a parent or guardian. Taxes on the prize are the sole responsibility of the winner. Odds of winning depend on the number of completed entries received. Enter as often as you wish, but each entry must be mailed separately. Bantam Books is not responsible for lost, misdirected or incomplete entries.

4. The sweepstakes is open to residents of the U.S. and Canada, except the Province of Quebec, and is void where prohibited by law. If the winner is a Canadian he/she will be required to correctly answer a skill question in order to receive the prize. All federal, state and local regulations apply. Employees of Reliable Travel International, The Delta Queen Steamboat Co., and Bantam, Doubleday, Dell Publishing Group, Inc., their subsidiary and affiliates, and their immediate families are ineligible to enter.

5. The winner may be required to submit an Affidavit of Eligibility and Promotional Release supplied by Bantam Books. The winner's name and likeness may be used for publicity purposes without additional compensation.

6. For an extra copy of the Official Rules and Entry Form, send a self-addressed stamped envelope (Washington and Vermont Residents need not affix postage) by June 15, 1988 to:

Bantam Books
Delaneys, THE UNTAMED YEARS Sweepstakes
Dept. HBG
666 Fifth Avenue
New York, NY 10103

OFFICIAL ENTRY FORM
DELANEYS, THE UNTAMED YEARS
MISSISSIPPI QUEEN' RIVERBOAT CRUISE SWEEPSTAKES

Name _____

Address _____

City _____ State _____ Zip Code _____

SW10

THE DELANEY DYNASTY

Men and women whose loves and passions are so glorious it takes many great romance novels by three bestselling authors to tell their tempestuous stories.

THE SHAMROCK TRINITY

☐ 21786 RAFE, THE MAVERICK
    by Kay Hooper $2.75
☐ 21787 YORK, THE RENEGADE
    by Iris Johansen $2.75
☐ 21788 BURKE, THE KINGPIN
    by Fayrene Preston $2.75

THE DELANEYS OF KILLAROO

☐ 21872 ADELAIDE, THE ENCHANTRESS
    by Kay Hooper $2.75
☐ 21873 MATILDA, THE ADVENTURESS
    by Iris Johansen $2.75
☐ 21874 SYDNEY, THE TEMPTRESS
    by Fayrene Preston $2.75

☐ 26991 THIS FIERCE SPLENDOR
    by Iris Johansen $3.95

THE DELANEYS: *The Untamed Years*

☐ 21897 GOLDEN FLAMES *by Kay Hooper* $3.50
☐ 21898 WILD SILVER *by Iris Johansen* $3.50
☐ 21999 COPPER FIRE *by Fayrene Preston* $3.50

Buy these books at your local bookstore or use the handy coupon below.

- -

Bantam Books, Dept. SW9, 414 East Golf Road, Des Plaines, IL 60016

Please send me the books I have checked above. I am enclosing $_____ (please add $2.00 to cover postage and handling). Send check or money order—no cash or C.O.D.s please.

Mr/Ms _____

Address _____

City/State _____ Zip _____

SW9—5/88

Please allow four to six weeks for delivery. This offer expires 11/88. Prices and availability subject to change without notice.